D0983816

GREEN
DRAGON CODEX

Books by R.D. Henham

RED DRAGON CODEX

BRONZE DRAGON CODEX

BLACK DRAGON CODEX

BRASS DRAGON CODEX

GREEN DRAGON CODEX

SILVER DRAGON CODEX
September 2009

GOLD DRAGON CODEX
January 2010

GREEN
DRAGON CODEX

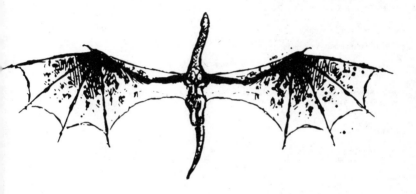

R.D. Henham

MIRRORSTONE®

Green Dragon Codex
©2009 Wizards of the Coast LLC

Text by R.D. Henham with assistance from Clint Johnson
Cover art by Vinod Rams
Interior art by Todd Lockwood
Cartography by Dennis Kauth
First Printing: June 2009

9 8 7 6 5 4 3 2 1

Library of Congress Cataloging-in-Publication Data

Henham, R. D.
  Green dragon codex / R.D. Henham.
    p. cm.
    Summary: Thirteen-year-old Scamp, his older brother Mather, and friend Dannika, pursued by evil-doers, set out to find someone who can protect the mysterious globe and tablet Scamp found next to the corpse of a dreaded green dragon.
  ISBN 978-0-7869-5145-1
  [1. Dragons--Fiction. 2. Fantasy.] I. Title.

PZ7.H3884Gre 2009
[Fic]--dc22

                                                                    2008048047

ISBN: 978-0-7869-5145-1
620-24053720-001-EN

U.S., CANADA,   EUROPEAN HEADQUARTERS
ASIA, PACIFIC, & LATIN AMERICA   Hasbro UK Ltd
Wizards of the Coast LLC   Caswell Way
P.O. Box 707   Newport, Gwent NP9 0YH
Renton, WA 98057-0707   GREAT BRITAIN
+1-800-324-6496   Save this address for your records.

Visit our Web site at www.mirrorstonebooks.com

For Master Astinus, who knows that even the simplest story is a great work.

—R.D.H.

For Casen, who reminds me that everything is magical.

—C.J.

Dear Honored Scribe Henham,

After all the trouble I put your poor, determined messenger through to locate me during my travels, I'm delighted to tell you that he discovered me investigating my next dragon story at a circus in the south of Solamnia. He's currently enjoying the jesters and snacking on roasted nuts while awaiting my next letter.

I'll tell you more about the circus and what transpired here next time, as my companions and I just discovered an incredible story about a green dragon. Green dragons, being of the chromatic persuasion, are often assumed to be horribly evil— and I can tell you from experience that the last green dragon I met was indeed quite rude.

But being both a kender and a wizard—a combination most people seem to think makes about as much sense as chocolate-coated monkfish (which

actually sounds like it might taste quite interesting!)—
I am not someone who judges books by their covers!
Neither was a boy named Scamp, who stumbled upon
a freshly hatched green dragon and decided to give it
a chance instead of declaring it evil from the start.

There's a whole lot of fun and surprises to this
particular tale. Dragons in disguise! A mysterious
ancient tablet! A desperate trek across Abanasinia!
And of course the question of whether a chromatic
dragon can ever actually be good. Oh, there's so much
fun and so many surprises that I can hardly stand it!

As always, my notes are enclosed for your
reading pleasure. I'll send them back with
your messenger—right after we get done watching
the acrobats on the flying trapeze!

All my best,

Sindri Suncatcher

A kender whose book doesn't match his cover

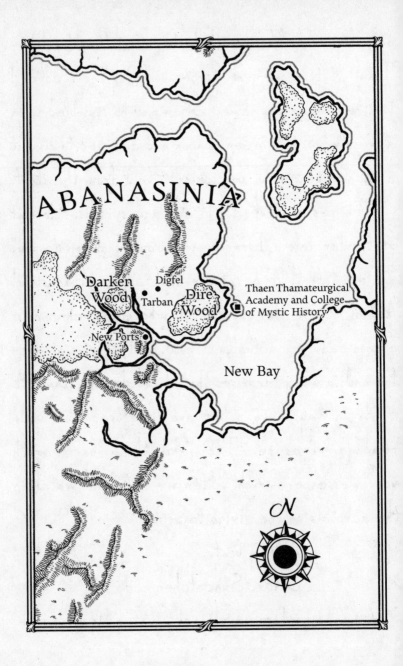

ABANASINIA

Darken
Wood   Digfel
        Tarban   Dire
                    Wood   Thaen Thamateurgical
                                  Academy and College
New Ports   of Mystic History

                        New Bay

N

PROLOGUE

Viressus finally tracked down the kidnappers in an ancient city of the ogres. The city was little more than shattered blocks and crags of granite with occasional pillars stabbing skyward like tips of bone from the earth. Through this skeleton walked the dragonslayers. They wore the armor of her kin's skin, red and white and blue and black and green. She thought once more of her slain mate, left to rot in their lair.

They would not have her child as well.

Viressus was in human form and wore a matching set of the horrid armor she'd taken from one of the murderers she'd found in her lair. Wearing the armor made her sick with rage and disgust, but she suppressed these feelings. She had to find her baby, and with the helm to disguise her, she could walk among the dragonslayers undiscovered.

There were dozens of them, mostly men, milling about and talking and laughing with each other at their crimes. Then a horn sounded, deep and mournful, from the center of the ruined city. The dragonslayers immediately walked quickly toward the call, as if whatever was happening had been long awaited.

The mother followed.

The procession led her to the shattered remains of some ancient temple. Only one wall stood, its flaking carvings too eroded to make out other than that they once must have been magnificent. Standing in front of the temple wall, as if it were the backdrop of a stage, was a black robed wizard. Seeing him, the mother's insides ached with fear for her missing unhatched child.

The Black Robe raised his arms, and the gathered dragonslayers went silent. "Bring me our prize," he said, barely whispering.

The throng of armor-clad men parted and two brought forward a chest. Viressus's heart thundered when she saw it, for she knew what lay inside—her stolen baby.

The pair of men carried the mahogany chest to the remains of the ancient altar and lay it reverently atop the stone.

"Open it," the wizard ordered.

Before the pair could obey, Viressus approached the altar. The dragonslayers watched her curiously, wondering why one of their own would act so oddly. But they did not try to stop her. Only the mage looked suspicious and alarmed.

"Why do you step forward unordered?" he demanded.

"To take back my stolen child," she answered. The

pair of dragonslayers who had carried the chest looked at her quizzically. Before they could do more than that, she growled—a sound deeper and more powerful than any human voice could produce—and grabbed them both by their breastplates. She lifted them from the ground as if they were straw dolls and hurled them away from the altar to crash into blocks of broken stone.

The Black Robe's eyes flared, and for a moment Viressus believed she saw a flicker of red, as if there were coals hidden behind his pupils. "You!" he shouted.

Snarling, she grabbed the chest and swung it with all her inhuman might into the evil man's chest. The mahogany was good and strong, and the impact lifted the frail wizard off his feet and sent him hurtling through the air. His robes flapped about him as he sped over the lip of a ragged cliff.

While the dragonslayers looked on stunned, Viressus threw open the chest. When she saw the egg inside and unhurt, she almost wept from joy. But there was no time for that. Speaking so quickly that she almost ruined the spells, she laid her hands on her precious egg, the last residue of family she had left. The egg crackled and glowed with magic, and she felt the shell harden to unyielding stone. Whether the rest of the magic took or not, she had no time to tell. The shock of seeing their master killed had worn off, and the dragonslayers were surging for her and their prize.

Time to be introduced formally.

Tugging off the hated helm, she hurled it at the nearest slayer. He batted it away with his sword, smirking as his fellows surrounded her. But then his cruel grin died.

Viressus's body, lean and soft as a human's, began to grow. The armor around her split, shedding like skin. The fragile, pale human flesh turned to plated scales of vibrant green. The mother, a massive green dragon once more, looked down on the murderers as if they were insects.

Most humans would have run screaming at the magnificent sight of her true form. Not these men. They were slayers, not just in name but in blood. They had killed her mate, and if she didn't escape soon, they would kill her as well. And her child. That was all they lived for—to slay dragons. And whatever aid the Black Robe had offered these men, her instinct told her it would produce a slaughter never seen in the history of dragonkind.

Before the dragonslayers could surround her completely, the mother Green exhaled chlorine gas, whipping her neck back and forth to spray in all directions. As men fell over themselves to flee the poison cloud, she grabbed the chest and leaped into the air. Two great beats of her wings and she was rising, flying free with her unhatched child safely in her grasp.

When she was high enough to know she was safe, she glanced back at the ground, hoping to find dozens of the hateful humans lying dead from her breath. What she saw instead nearly knocked her from the sky.

The Black Robe stood atop the altar, unharmed. Even from high above, she saw that his eyes did indeed glow red with dark power and hate. Pointing to her as if the gesture could strike her from the sky, he cried, "Stop her, Great One, or your vengeance is lost!"

The earth shook from a great and furious roar. It was a cry Viressus knew, a dragon's call, but louder and stronger than her own voice. The hillside rumbled and ancient blocks toppled away from the bronze dragon as it shot out from a cave at the hill's base.

The mother flew as hard and fast as she could, fearing it would not be enough. Cradling the chest and its precious egg inside, she prayed to any god who would listen, light or dark, to save her child.

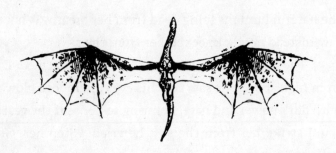

CHAPTER 1

As usual, Scamp was hiding.

This was often the case. Whether he was ducking chores or avoiding Madam Billings after sampling her fresh baked goods, a large part of his thirteen years had been spent tucked away in some nook or cranny, trying to avoid something. Normally, this didn't bother him. Being alone a lot seemed a fair trade for missing chores or snatching an odd marmalade crisp off the baker's window.

Today, however, was an exception. Today, there wasn't one thing he liked about hiding. First, he was in the loft of Trigneth Duncan's barn. Duncan couldn't cobble together two twigs to make a stick, and his barn roof leaked buckets, so the hay Scamp huddled in was sopping wet from the morning's rain. The second reason was that once again, Jaiben was after him.

This was a good hiding spot, though. Good enough to lay low and let Jaiben and his pack—

"Hey! There he is!" The cry came from below. The voice

was loud and mad and somehow sounded fat. Jaiben.

Scamp heard the creak of Duncan's rickety ladder. Someone was climbing. Without looking to spot his pursuer, Scamp leaped up. He plowed through hay stacked up to his waist.

"It's him! Jaiben, he's up there," another voice called. The other boys were all over the barn floor.

Jaiben's face, round and freckled and pink cheeked from climbing and fury, peeked over the ladder into the loft. Scamp glanced at the other boy's green-stained hair and grinned. Jaiben's scowl deepened. "Found you, Scamp. I'm going to mash your nose so flat . . . hey!"

Scamp changed direction and sprinted to the loft door, then leaped out. After a moment in the air, almost flying, he reached the rope Duncan used to lift hay into the loft. Scamp swung in a great circle and landed against the wall with his feet. Scurrying down the rope like a squirrel, he was on the ground in no time. He could still hear voices inside the barn yelling, wondering what had happened to him.

"Mash my nose." Scamp laughed. "Not this time, green bean."

He turned and nearly bumped noses with Jaiben's friend Chester. For a moment Scamp stared at the bully's tiny, close-set eyes, too surprised to run. He never got a second chance to flee. Chester clenched his fist and punched

Scamp hard in the belly. Scamp doubled over and fell into the mud, all breath driven from his lungs. It felt like he'd swallowed a nail.

"Jaiben," Chester called, "I got him! He's over here, I got him!"

In moments Scamp was surrounded by all four boys, each bigger than he was and scowling promises. They pounded their fists together, eager to retaliate for Jaiben's dyed-green hair.

Jaiben towered over Scamp, who was still trying to breathe on the ground. The bully's head looked like a raggedy fern. "You ruined my hat," he growled.

No, *my* hat, Scamp thought. A few days ago he'd dropped it while running from the bullies, and Jaiben had claimed it as a trophy. Anger bubbled in Scamp's gut. But he tried to look innocent.

"Sorry, Jaiben," he said. "Your hat looked a little dull. I thought it could use a bit of sprucing up—you know, a touch of paint."

Jaiben's scowl deepened. "You put the paint inside the hat."

Scamp furrowed his brow. "Are you sure you put it on right? Up, down, we've gone over this so many times already—"

Before he'd finished speaking he rolled to his feet and began to run. It was a quick motion, but not quick enough.

Jaiben's hand caught his shirt and tugged him off his feet. The bully's fat fist wrenched the shirt tight around Scamp's neck like a noose. He was forced to stand on tiptoe to keep from choking, and even then his eyes watered from the pressure on his throat.

"What do you think, fellas?" Jaiben asked his gang. "Do we let him off with a beating, or do we shave him?"

"Shave him!" the others cried eagerly.

"Then beat him," Chester added.

Jaiben grinned. "Right." He shook Scamp. "Someone get me a knife."

Scamp started to struggle. It hurt his neck and pulled his shirt tighter, but he didn't care. He didn't trust Jaiben with a knife. He didn't trust that the bully would cut only hair. Once, Scamp had told his mother he thought Jaiben was half ogre. That explained why he was so mean, not to mention so ugly. She'd sent him to his room with a heel of bread for supper and a warning never to say such things again.

"Let me go!" He started beating at Jaiben's arm, trying to break free. Jaiben just watched, grinning. The others laughed. Scamp looked at the bully's yellow teeth and thought, Tusks. I knew it. Ogre. "Let go!"

"What is this?" The voice came from somewhere to Scamp's left. It was a voice Scamp knew well—Mather's.

For anyone but Scamp, an older brother showing up

at a time like this would have been a good thing. A great thing. Mather was, well, mostly what Scamp wasn't. At sixteen, he was as big as most men in the village, tall with broad shoulders and thick arms. He was the only boy in Tarban whose muscles you could see, and point to them and pick out the different parts. People said he and Scamp looked alike, but Scamp didn't agree. They both had brown hair. But where Scamp's eyes were the same dull brown as his hair, Mather's were biting green. Mather had eyes that made you know when he was looking at you.

Mather was looking at the bullies then, and from their expressions Scamp knew they no longer believed they had the advantage of either size or number. Jaiben alone kept the same cocky scowl.

"I asked what's going on," Mather said. He walked into Scamp's view, appraising the situation sternly.

"Look at my hair," Jaiben demanded. He grabbed a handful of his green hair. It looked like someone trying to pull carrots out of the ground.

Mather did look. Then he looked at Scamp. The touch of that green gaze felt like the tip of an icicle. "Did you do this?" His tone made it clear he assumed the answer was yes.

"It was an accident," Scamp managed to say despite the shirt strangling his throat.

Mather sighed and continued to look at Scamp. He

looked long and hard and sternly, showing no pity, no sadness, nothing but judgment and disappointment. It was the look Scamp had been expecting. Still, it hurt to know that once again, his brother was not on his side.

"You started this, Scamp." Mather did not walk away, but he made no move to protect Scamp.

Jaiben grinned, nodding at his companions, who laughed in return. In the distance a door slammed shut. Chester was bringing Jaiben his knife.

"They're going to shave me, Mather," he pleaded. "They're going to cut me."

"So fight back," the older boy said.

If he hadn't been hanging by his shirt, Scamp might have fought—not Jaiben or the bullies, but Mather. He would have lost badly, but it would have been worth it. Mather always told him to fight back. It made sense if you were big and strong and could wrestle a wolf till its fur came off. It made sense if you were Mather. Scamp, on the other hand, knew that any fight he took part in he'd probably lose. Why fight if you couldn't win?

"So you're just going to sit there and watch?" Scamp asked.

"I can't always protect you," Mather said.

"You never protect me," Scamp retorted. Shifting his gaze to Jaiben, he said, "And I do fight back, don't I, bean brain?"

Before Jaiben could answer, Scamp pulled in his legs, putting all his weight on the bully's arm. Strong as he was, Jaiben dropped him. Scamp tugged off his boot as the bully tried to grab his shirt once more. Holding it in both hands as if it were a flimsy hammer, he swung it hard into the side of Jaiben's head. The bully tottered back, windmilled his arms, and fell in a puddle.

Before Jaiben's angry pack could retaliate, Scamp kicked off his other boot and ran.

CHAPTER 2

Scamp ran for the edge of the village and the forest some distance beyond. He could hear Jaiben behind him, ordering the others to chase him.

As soon as Scamp reached the tree line, he wove around the trunks, swung around branches and slid down hills. The bullies, not nearly as nimble, crashed through the growth like charging rams.

As he led them deeper into the woods, he dared one glance over his shoulder. Most of the bullies were floundering, holding scraped faces or sitting on the ground where they'd slipped. Jaiben alone continued the chase. He was a horse length or two behind, running with his head lowered, as if ready to gore Scamp like a bull.

Scamp decided to let him hit something else instead.

Seeing a perfect branch ahead, Scamp caught it with both hands. His momentum bent the branch in a large, tight arc. As soon as it was at full bend he dropped to the ground. Sliding through the mud, he watched the branch whip through the air, then collide into the center of Jaiben's lowered head. The bully's head rocked back as his body continued forward, spinning him in the air like a top fallen off a table. He hit the forest floor, kicking up waves of rotting leaves.

Scamp didn't wait to see if Jaiben would get up or not. Instead, he scrambled down a hill and into the gulch where he had been heading the whole time. The Bristly Briar.

Despite the name, the briar wasn't a collection of nettles or thorny plants, but a huge growth of steelstring. The steelstring plant was unique because it was all root, no leaves, no bough, no stem or flower. Just shoot after shoot, thick as arms, of tendril roots that spread in all directions, even up at the sky, searching for water, rotting vegetation, and better soil. When many of these plants congregated in one place—such as in the briar—they began a huge wrestling match. Strands from one plant would entwine with others, forming loops and whirls and pithy knots. In some places the plants even merged. The effect was a structure something like a giant spiderweb with hard, living wood. The resulting tangle was completely impassable.

For everyone but Scamp, that is.

When he reached the briar, Scamp began to climb where others would stop—not up, but in, toward the heart of the tangle. He wedged his lithe body through gaps barely large enough for a squirrel.

Once he reached the center of the briar, he sat on a particularly fat root and looked back. He could barely see the forest past the tangle. Breathing heavily, he felt a strong sense of satisfaction. No one could follow him in here. Jaiben wouldn't even try. If he so much as poked his fat chin in the tangle, he would get stuck.

Part of Scamp was still angry—not sad, of course— that once again, Mather hadn't come to his aid when he needed him. But from the briar it seemed a small trouble, much like the bullies themselves. They couldn't hurt him here. No one and nothing could.

No sooner had he thought this than the sun went out. Then just for a moment, he became aware of a color— green. It filled everything, and with it came a deafening roar that sounded like all the mountains on Krynn collapsing at once.

There was a tremendous crash and something batted him off his perch and through the air. Bits of steelstring cut and pricked his skin as he spun through a world dissolved to blurred brown and forest green. He barely had time to wonder how far he had to fall when he jolted to a stop.

Splintered wood rained down around him. Gradually, the bombardment lessened, then stopped. Scamp didn't know if that was because no more wood was falling or if he'd been buried so deep that he couldn't feel the impact anymore. Despite being buried alive, he managed to keep calm and think. The terrible sound, like a stone screeching as it was ground to dust, had stopped. Whatever had happened out there was over, Scamp guessed. Now to find out where he was.

Considering how far he must have fallen, his landing had been surprisingly soft. He discovered why when he started to dig around in the material covering him. Leaves. Some were wet from rain, others crisp and moldering, showing that they'd been decomposing for some time.

Feeling lucky and wondering what in the names of the gods had happened, Scamp dug his way free. Soon his head popped out of the litter. He rubbed his eyes and looked around.

Half of the briar was gone, smashed to kindling and scattered throughout the surrounding forest. In place of the fractured shrubbery lay a massive hillock of green shale-like plates. The gods hadn't dropped a mountain—one had grown straight up from the ground under him.

Then Scamp saw one of the green flakes lying by his face. He picked it up and as he felt it, he suddenly understood.

It wasn't stone. It was a scale. A glossy, green scale as big as his palm.

He looked at the hill in awe. No, not a hill—a dragon.

Now that he knew what he was seeing, he could make out the shape of its body. It was the largest thing he'd ever seen, he was sure, bigger than any barn. That curl there was its tail, folding in on itself at the far side of the clearing. The lump in front of him was a hind leg, big as a horse. He could just make out the glint of giant claws, ivory spikes long as large daggers. And to his right, at the end of a snakelike neck bent into an arc, was the head.

Scamp stood up. He didn't wipe away clinging leaves or shake tepid water off. He didn't even notice these things. All he could see was the incredible creature lying before him. The dragon's head was longer than he was tall. Wedge-shaped and scaled, it reminded him partially of a lizard or snake, but also of a giant predatory cat. Something in the lines, in the streamlined nature, hinted at great grace combined with magnificent power. The entire form was lean muscle by the ton, made to run, and jump, and . . .

Fly.

His gaze traced one huge wing from the body to its very tip, which lay almost within Scamp's reach. The membrane of the wing, surprisingly thin for such a massive beast, was in tatters. Lengths of broken steelstring stabbed through the membrane by the dozens. Scamp suddenly felt that this wonderful creature, born to soar, had been nailed to the dirt.

Then he smelled the blood. He didn't know why he hadn't noticed before. As soon as he looked it became obvious. The ground was slick with red. There was so much it had puddled in places, gathering like rainwater in the mud. The air stank of metal and gore.

Scamp looked at the dragon's head again, and the beauty and awe he'd felt at his initial glance was gone. Now he noticed deep gashes in the body, patches of missing scales, and what looked to be burn or scorch marks in several places. The neck, so long and fragile compared to the great bulk of the body, had a sharp kink in the center— it was broken.

The dragon was dead.

This was more impossible to believe than actually seeing a real dragon. But it was true. The dragon was dead.

What was he going to do? He had to tell someone. But who? Mather? No chance. His brother would find some way to blame Scamp for it. His parents? They were still in Haven trading for supplies. He could show neighbors, but what then? How would people respond if they knew the dragons hadn't really left, as everyone claimed? There were still plenty of people who remembered how the evil dragonarmies left Haven, Solace, and all the other towns in ashes. Scamp still had nightmares about smoke and fire occasionally.

And what to do with the dragon itself? At the very least it deserved to be buried or burned, some kind of tribute. He looked at the scale in his hand, thin but hard as steel. A green scale. Green dragons were evil. They had fought for the dragonarmies in the war—not as many as the Blues or Reds, but a few. That this dragon was dead was probably a good thing.

Still, a creature so magnificent deserved better than to rot on the forest floor.

Scamp's troubled thoughts were interrupted by a sound in the distance. At first he mistook it for a gust of wind, only it didn't die down. In fact, it grew louder the longer he listened. Soon the deep thumping was so loud he could place it: huge beating wings above the tree line to his left.

Another dragon.

Fear, which he had not had time to experience with the arrival of the first dragon, gripped him. He imagined another creature like the one laid out before him, only alive and angry, and maybe eager to snack on a boy not wise enough to run away when he'd had the chance.

Scamp dived into what remained of the Bristly Briar. He moved through the knotted wood without his usual grace, scraping his skin on rough bark, bruising his hands and shoulders from forcing his way through the snarl. Anything to get deeper, away from the rising roar of displaced air that cast up a cloud of dirt and leaves and blood.

He huddled in the dirt and looked up as molten metal and the roaring force of a hurricane filled the sky.

If the green dragon was larger than anything he'd ever seen, this dragon was too large even to imagine. It filled the sky, its wings so wide he couldn't glimpse their ends in the clearing. Its scales were a radiant bronze that reflected the sunlight like mirrors. The dragon was so large he suspected it could carry a draft horse in each claw and still fly with no problems.

The dragon observed the body of its fallen foe. Its head snaked back and forth atop a long neck as the beating wings kept its massive body hovering above the trees. It looked to be searching for something. Scamp huddled even lower in the dirt.

"I cannot land. The clearing is not large enough," said someone above him.

Scamp was stunned to realize it was the dragon who had spoken. Its voice was deep and resonant, like the vibrating of a great drum, yet something in the sound was pleasant, almost musical.

"Hold steady," a man's voice answered. There were riders on the dragon.

As the dragon hovered above the clearing, a rope spiraled to the ground. A pair of armored figures descended the line. The warriors were completely hidden by their armor, which bore an intricate design of overlapping scales done in myriad colors. Scamp saw red plates overlapping blue, and green and black and white, scattered in a rainbow hue.

Struck by the similarity, Scamp looked at the scale he held. It matched the green plates.

The armor wasn't iron or steel. These men wore dragon hide.

When they landed on the ground, the pair drew long-bladed swords and spread out. Ignoring the dead dragon, they searched the ground, digging through the piles of green scales with their blades. They were looking for something. One of the warriors was even studying the remainder of the briar itself—Scamp's hiding place.

These men had killed the dragon. The thought brought Scamp a feeling of awe, almost reverence. Maybe these men were Solamnic Knights, the heroes who had defeated the dragonarmies. Maybe even the Heroes of the Lance! He felt a strong urge to leap up, yell, and wave his arms, just to be noticed by such men.

Instead, he kept hidden. Maybe he was being over-cautious. But if growing up in war had taught Scamp one thing, it was never to trust strangers with weapons.

Looking for a route to slip away on without being spotted, he found something else instead—a chest.

It was suspended above him, caught in the crux of three intertwined steelstring roots. It was made of smooth, dark mahogany that seemed to shrug off light. It had thick iron hinges and a lock as big as his fist. Scamp had no doubt this was what the men were searching for.

"Maybe the Green crushed it," one soldier called.

The other warrior stuck his head into the tangled briar. Scamp could feel his gaze lancing from the dark slit in the helm. Cringing behind a clump of roots, he prayed to any god who would listen—new or old—that he would not be found.

Frustrated, the dragonslayer tried to withdraw from the briar. The roots caught his helm, nearly pulling it off his head. Straightening the troublesome piece of armor, the man swore and hacked at the briar. The blade severed several roots. Without the intervening support, the surrounding roots collapsed, becoming even tighter and more tangled.

"We'll never find it in this," the man said.

"You can cut your way through," the dragon said. Its voice boomed more loudly than the men's, even from so far above. "Hurry. We cannot— Beware the Green!"

Scamp stared at the dead dragon in confusion. Beware what? Then he glimpsed a strange, yellowish mist rising from the body. It looked to be venting from two holes in the dragon's side, one blackened and charred as if by fire.

As Scamp watched, the mist began to seep along the ground. Beneath it, leaves wilted and curled in on themselves, darkening to gray, then black.

"The beast's breath," one warrior said. They both retreated from the dragon's body.

"Climb back up," the dragon ordered.

"What of the chest?" It was not an argument, as both warriors had already returned to the rope and begun to climb.

"We will return and find it once the poison has dissipated," the dragon answered. "For now, I must rest. My wound makes flying difficult."

For the first time Scamp noticed a trio of gashes in the dragon's flank, where scales had been torn free. Blood trickled from the long wounds like water from melting ice.

The warriors were once more on the dragon's back, forcing Scamp to strain to hear what they said. "Are you sure it survived?" one warrior asked. "If we were to lose it, the plan would fall to nothing."

"It survives. The gods' justice would not let it be otherwise," the Bronze growled. "This will help us find it when we return."

Opening its huge maw, the dragon drew in a long breath. Its body swelled. Then, with a crack like a thunderbolt, blinding light streaked from its mouth to the very center of the briar.

The lightning tore through the briar and hit the earth in a tremendous explosion. Scamp flew backward as bits of blazing steelstring fell around him. As he got to his feet, he found the entire briar was on fire.

With a roar that made his bones shiver, the dragon wheeled in the sky and disappeared, winging east. Scamp was left alone with the sun setting, its light being replaced by that of the quickly growing blaze.

Scamp managed to keep ahead of the spreading flame as he wove his way through the briar. Finally, he stepped out into the open. Away from the flames and the dragon's corpse, which was still leaking vapor into the air, he told himself to run home, jump in bed, and forget this had ever happened.

But he couldn't.

He couldn't forget the men in dragon armor, or the dragons themselves. Most of all, he couldn't forget the chest.

Peering into the briar that was now half consumed in flame, Scamp saw the chest lying in the mud. What was in it? Some great weapon or magical relic? Maybe this was the dragon's treasure? He imagined opening the chest to find it full of steel coins, thousands of them, and of showing the hoard to his parents. He pictured their faces and Mather's as they saw the wealth and realized that their problems were over. They could move away from Abanasinia, away from this land of ashy fields and razed villages. They could start real lives, where war wasn't even a memory.

Eyeing the chest—and the wall of flame steadily rising around it—Scamp dived back into the burning briar before he could think better of it.

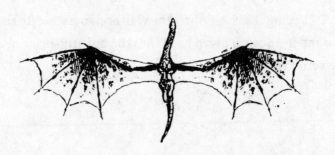

CHAPTER 3

Scamp dropped the rough pine poles of the litter and groaned, marveling that his arms hadn't dropped with them. That chest wasn't so heavy when he first lifted it, but after more than a mile, it felt like he had dragged home the whole dragon, rather than the chest. Hiding the chest for long enough to open it would be tricky, though. He'd never have managed a dragon. Leaving the litter in the dirt, Scamp crept to a thicket at the edge of the village to try to determine a way to get the chest home unseen.

It didn't take long for him to spot possible help. Dannika Shellkeep, Scamp's best if often irritating friend, stood in the village square—which was a patch of dirt and desiccated grass—watching the sun creep near the purple tops of the Kharolis Mountains. Scamp examined her lips, which were pressed to a thin, dark line. That wasn't good. She was mad. Maybe worried, but probably mad. And probably at him.

Still, she was likely the only help he was going to

26

get who wouldn't turn him in before he got a chance to see inside the chest. He was about to call to her when she spoke out instead.

Fixing her gaze on the horizon, her eyes widened. "Fire," she said so breathlessly Scamp barely heard her. Then, loud enough for the whole village to hear, "Fire! Fire!"

The village burst into activity like a kicked anthill. People streamed out of their doorways, running to the east end of the village to watch the glow spread across the darkened sky. Scamp listened to the adults talk in tense, worried voices and wonder at the nature of the flames. He nestled down a little deeper in the brush and reminded himself the fire wasn't his fault. Even though true, it didn't make him feel much better—just as it wouldn't reassure the villagers.

Tarban, like many other villages in Abanasinia, had grown up from a refugee camp during the war. Every person in the village had seen towns burned, both in person and from a distance. Everyone in Tarban had similar stories: how the blazes would make the sky glow, then blot out the color with oily smoke. Thus they all watched the blush of crimson spread across the sky and drown out the stars, hoping the sign was not ominous.

"What's going on?"

Scamp didn't dare breathe, despite his hiding place, as Mather came running from their home to see why Dannika had called out. Great, just what he needed. The moment his brother saw the chest, he would demand Scamp return it to where he found it. As if that wasn't bad enough, then would come questions about the dragons and warriors and the fire painting the sky red, and Mather would come to the same conclusion he always arrived at: it was all Scamp's fault.

Settling into his hiding place, Scamp pondered what to do. As he thought, he listened.

When Mather approached her, Dannika pointed to the lit sky. "Something started a fire. Where's Scamp?"

Mather's mouth tightened to a grim line. "I don't know, but I can guess." He glared at the glow on the horizon.

"Don't joke like that. Not about this."

"I wasn't joking," he said sternly.

"Scamp wouldn't trick with fire," she said. "Even he wouldn't do that, and you know it."

"I know that he does things and things happen to him," Mather answered. "Either way, he's always in the middle."

Dannika offered no defense on Scamp's behalf, and Scamp returned the favor with a silent yet wicked scowl. "You don't think he's over there, do you?" she asked.

Mather just stared at the growing blaze. His eyes reflected the light, turning orange and showing nothing of what he may have been feeling.

"Jaiben's worse than a hobgoblin," she snapped. "If

Scamp gets hurt I'll do worse than rap that bully's noggin—I'll crack it." She looked ready to cry, which made Scamp feel sorry about the scowl. Instead, she wheeled on Mather. "And you. Why don't you ever stick up for him?"

"Scamp needs to learn to take care of himself," Mather said coldly.

"And what says you can't help out now and then?" she asked. "You're his brother. That's your job."

"It's not," he said. "I won't be around to protect him any more than Father is. If he causes trouble he needs to solve it. One of these day's he'll have to learn to stand up and be a man. At least, he will if you don't keep doing it for him."

"Are you calling me a man?"

He didn't even look at her. "No, just more of one than Scamp. That isn't saying much."

"Someday Scamp's going to prove you wrong," she said. Once she'd spoken the words she looked at the ground and shuffled her feet, as if she felt foolish.

Watching her, Scamp felt that raw ache of inferiority throb inside him, reminding him that something was missing. It hurt, but he couldn't really blame his friend for feeling foolish at taking his side. Betting on him to show up Mather? Even he had to admit that was doubtful.

Mather's expression made it clear that he felt the same. "Maybe. But I think the prospect unlikely."

As he often did, Scamp acted without thinking.

Snatching a piece of burned twig stuck in his hair, he hurled it at his brother. It spun through the darkness and hit Mather on the cheek.

"What in the gods' graces?"

Kneeling down, Mather examined the piece of charred wood that had hit him.

"Where did that come from?" Dannika asked.

In answer, Scamp giggled and shook the bush in which he hid, making it shiver. When both of them looked, he popped his head up and offered his most innocent smile.

"Scamp," Mather growled. He broke the burned stick.

"Where have you been?" Dannika demanded. She sounded ready to switch him.

"Come here!" Scamp waved to them without leaving the bush. "Hurry!"

Still scowling at him pointedly, Dannika did as he asked. After a moment, Mather followed, the broken twig still in hand.

As they rounded the bush they both froze to gawk at him. He looked from one to the other, wondering why they were staring.

Mather looked at his brother in disgust. "You're perverse."

"What? Why?" Scamp asked. He looked down at himself and saw he was covered head to toe in soot, wearing nothing but his underpants and boots. He'd used his shirt and pants to make the litter, and he'd totally forgotten! Looking up, he saw Dannika staring at him with her mouth open. When she realized he was watching her stare, she quickly looked away. It was the first time Scamp had ever seen her dark skin blush.

"You're bare as a satyr!" Mather exclaimed.

"Oh, that. I needed them to make the litter." Motioning for the pair to follow, Scamp walked farther into the forest until he reached the makeshift litter. The carrying device was made of two thick branches with his shirt and pants wrapped around them to create a sling. Sitting in the middle of the sling was the chest.

Dannika studied the chest—and pointedly did not look at Scamp. "Where did you find it?"

"In the forest," he answered.

"And who does it belong to?" Mather demanded.

"Search me." Folding his arms across his bare chest, Scamp grinned.

His older brother scowled. "Take it back."

"I said I don't know whose it is," Scamp said. He knelt beside the chest before Mather could ask any further questions. "Maybe we can find something inside to tell us who it belongs to when we open it."

"We aren't opening anything," Mather said.

Ignoring him, Scamp looked around. His gaze focused on Dannika's hair. "Danni, can I borrow that comb?"

"Why?" she asked.

He waggled his fingers. "Just give it."

Sighing, she pulled the vallenwood comb from her hair. She shook her long braids over her shoulders and handed the comb to Scamp. "Be careful—"

He snapped two teeth off the comb.

"Hey!" she cried.

He didn't even glance at her. Focusing on the lock, he carefully inserted both teeth into the keyhole and began to jiggle them around. His tongue poked out from between his lips as he worked.

"Paladine, have mercy on the moronic," Mather said. "Where did you learn to do that?"

"Nettlebottom," Scamp said, still working at the lock.

"The kender!" Mather shook his head. "That's it. Now you'll end up in some dungeon for sure."

"I just want to. . . Hey!" The teeth snapped in half. He held them up before his face, as if glaring would make them whole again.

"That lock's too strong," said Dannika. "You won't be able to break it either, not without ruining what's inside." She snatched her comb and batted Scamp on the back of the head in payment for the missing teeth.

"Then how are we going to open it?" Scamp said. He gazed at the sturdy chest with longing.

"We're not. You're going to take it back," Mather said.

"I told you, I can't," Scamp insisted. "If we're going to find out who it belongs to we have to get inside."

They both looked at him as if he'd been caught in a lie. And all right, maybe it wasn't strictly true. But he had to know what was in that chest. He just had to! He probably wouldn't die from curiosity, but it certainly felt like it. Knowing better than to appeal to Mather, who was scowling again, Scamp put on his most pleading, pitiful expression and looked at Dannika.

The girl's wry expression told him she knew his game. He didn't care as long as it worked.

"I know where we can take it," she finally admitted. "Just stop looking at me like that!"

CHAPTER 4

Mather hoisted the chest onto his shoulder with Scamp's help, and the trio quickly moved westward out of the village, away from the fire spreading on the horizon.

The man they went to meet lived on the Westrich Ridge, so called because it was the only elevated ground within leagues of Tarban. The ridge was near enough to take part in town life but far enough to not be a part of town, which was just how Peda liked it.

Though his name was Peda, Dannika called him "Shal'het," which Scamp understood to mean a combination of "friend," "instructor," and "hero." Scamp would have added "god" to the list, as Dannika's fondness for Peda neared reverence. But he'd been warned against such blasphemy now that the gods were back. Thinking an angry god would be quite a bad thing, Scamp heeded this advice.

Mather winced beneath the weight of the chest. "How much farther?" he asked, puffing.

"Not far," Dannika answered.

As the forest thinned and the ground sloped upward, Peda's shack peeked out over the top of the hill. It was a modest structure but strong, made of whole cedar trunks laid one atop the other. The roof was thick thatch. Around the shack lay a clearing filled with a dozen flat-topped wooden posts driven deep into the ground. The posts protruded to different heights, from only a few hands high to taller than Scamp. They were a type of physical training equipment that Dannika called Harrow Steps. Peda had taught Dannika how to improve her balance and concentration by running up and down them and doing the strange hand waving and kicks she insisted was a fighting style.

Scamp tapped Dannika on the shoulder. "Come on, one quick contest!" Then he sprinted toward the posts. On his way, he passed a large circle target made of wood. The target face bristled with several darts, expertly fletched with turkey feathers. Snatching the darts, he gestured for Dannika to join him.

She scowled. "We didn't come here to play—"

"I thought you said this was serious practice?" he teased.

Her mouth thinned even more. "Why don't you go help your brother?"

Scamp looked down the hill and saw that Mather had set the chest on the ground. The older boy's chest was straining with heavy breathing, and he wiped his face with a tattered work cloth. Then grunting, he hoisted the heavy chest back up, resting it this time on his left shoulder. He stared sourly at Scamp the entire time.

"He's doing fine," Scamp said. "Besides, I offered to help him carry it and he wouldn't let me. He said I'd get lazy and drop my side and break both his legs."

"Would you?" she challenged.

"Probably. But I wouldn't mean to. Come on. Best out of three throws." Scamp hoisted himself on top of one of posts at the edge of the shorn-off orchard. The top of the post was so smooth that Scamp had to throw out his arms to avoid slipping off it. He almost dropped the darts he held in his hands.

Dannika had shown Scamp how to use the poles in hopes that he'd share her fascination and train with her. Unfortunately, she reacted poorly when he told her he wasn't interested in any training, but walking on the poles and tossing darts was no end of fun. Apparently, things that were good for you weren't supposed to be fun.

Dannika gave a strict shake of her head. "Get down and be serious."

"Look, I'll make it easy on you: I'll take three steps before the throw and you only have to take one. Deal?"

The glare she shot him made words unnecessary.

Sighing, he slumped his shoulders. Then he spun

around, jumped up three of the stumps, and turning smoothly on a heel, flicked his wrist. A dart whistled through the darkness and buried itself in the board. There was just enough light for him to see it sticking out of the target's bull's-eye, only a finger's width from the very center. Still standing on a single foot, he folded his arms and stuck his tongue out at her. "I would have won anyway."

Dannika approached the board to examine the shot. She bit her bottom lip.

Jumping off the post, he twirled once in the air and landed by her side. "See?"

"You are the most scatterbrained person I know," she said. "You shouldn't be able to do that. Worse, you do that without even being serious!"

"Showing joy does not mean one rejects wisdom." A lean silhouette appeared in the shack's doorway. "The truly wise have more reason to be joyous than all others."

Peda exited his home to stand before Dannika. That was all he did, stand and look at her, but the effect was startling. She immediately lowered her eyes, replacing the haughtiness of a moment before with deep respect. "Yes, Shal'het."

Scamp grinned. But his grin died when Peda said, "But have you ever wondered, young Scamp Weaver, if you would play so well if you realized it is no game?"

Scamp didn't understand what that meant—he almost

never understood Peda—and didn't know how to react, other than to feel sorry for his gloating.

"What have you brought me, young friends?" Peda asked.

Mather had finally reached the shack. Wincing, he fought to balance the chest as he lowered it from his shoulder. Without being asked, Peda took one end of the chest and helped lower it to the ground. The hermit was wiry and none too tall, but he handled his share of the weight easily. Scamp noted his brother's look of surprise and respect, for both were uncommon on that stubborn, implacable face.

"My thanks," Mather wheezed.

Peda bobbed his head, a small smile on his lips. When he ducked down, his hair fell forward, giving a glimpse of a pointed ear. Unlike most individuals of mixed heritage—and there were more than ever following the war—Peda expressed no shame in his family tree and did not try to hide it. Derived of a human druid and a Kagonesti elf, his looks borrowed from both his parents: strength and a solid physique from his human mother, and lithe dexterity and grace from his wild elf father.

In town, people talked of Peda frequently while denying doing so. Because of this, Scamp was fascinated with the hermit. That fascination had only increased when he met the man, though not nearly to the same degree as

Dannika's. What interested Scamp was this sense about Peda, a kind of orderliness. It even showed in the hermit's face. It wasn't his features exactly, which were thin and sharp. It was something else, beneath skin and deeper than bone. Scamp could describe it only as a peace.

Normally, the word "peace" would come with bushels full of bad feelings for Scamp. Whenever he heard it, people were saying, "Leave me in peace" or "keep your peace, boy" or something similar, and often screaming it. Normally, peaceful meant boring. Yet, for some reason he didn't understand, Scamp thought the kind of peace he saw in Peda's almond eyes wouldn't be quite so bad.

"I found this chest in the forest," Scamp said. "We were hoping you could—"

"Convince Scamp to give it back before someone brings him before the constable," Mather interrupted.

"If we are going to give it back," Scamp said smoothly, "we need to open it to see who it belongs to. Do you think you could?"

Scamp stopped speaking when Peda, who had reached out to examine the chest, froze. He stood with his hand outstretched, as if feeling something radiating from the chest. He almost looked to be warming his hands at a fire, but the expression on his face was anything but comfortable.

When Peda looked at Scamp, his face was sterner than the boy had ever seen it. "Where did you get this?"

Scamp didn't think about fudging the truth for more than an instant. "In the forest. It's . . . a dragon's chest."

Dannika and Mather gaped at him. "You mean we've run off with something that belongs to a dragon!" his brother bellowed.

Dannika hugged herself. "If it comes looking for it—"

"It wasn't a live dragon," Scamp stressed. "It was dead. I know, I saw it, and I just thought that if this was treasure, then maybe we could make everything better." He did not mention the warriors he'd seen, or the second dragon.

"Where did this happen?" Peda asked suspiciously, staring at the glow on the horizon.

"At the briar," Scamp admitted.

It was startling how quickly the half-elf moved. Grabbing Scamp and Dannika by the wrist, he tugged them toward the shack. "Inside, quickly!" He waved to Mather. "Help me take it inside. Now!"

Startled and a little frightened, Scamp did as he was asked. As soon as everyone was inside, Peda shut the door and bolted it. Scamp had the feeling that the door closed just in time, that something out in the darkness had chased them until the last sliver of light from the shack disappeared. He told himself he was trembling at shadows like a baby.

"What's the matter, Shal'het?" Dannika asked.

Peda helped Mather set the chest on a small table in the corner. "This chest hides something evil—it is full of hate and rage. But also sadness . . . such terrible sadness."

Mather edged away from the chest.

"So, we shouldn't open it?" Scamp said.

"I'm afraid that is no longer a choice." Peda looked at Scamp, not with blame but some other unidentifiable emotion. "Sometimes where our curiosity leads us, our courage must sustain us."

Peda focused on the chest intently. That gentle aura about him hardened and became so intense it could almost be seen. He rubbed his hands together slowly. Laying his thumb against the lock directly above the keyhole, he turned his wrist. A quiet *snick* sounded.

Scamp looked at Dannika, delighted. "That is the neatest thing I've ever seen!" he said.

"Thank the gods you can't do it," Mather muttered.

Peda opened the chest. Scamp practically stood on his toes trying to spy inside. He watched firelight invade the container to reveal a pair of items: a strange stone globe with a blotchy pattern on its surface, and a stone tablet with illegible markings across its face.

While the writing was intriguing, Scamp had never been too fond of reading, and the other item was so much more interesting because the shapes on the globe were moving. It was hard to see and he first thought it was a trick of the firelight, but no, the blotches on the globe were slowly swirling, as if smoke were trapped under the surface of the stone.

He couldn't help himself. Picking up the globe, he said, "Wow!"

"Put it down!" Mather insisted.

"Just a moment," Peda said. He reached for the globe himself but his hand stopped just short of touching it. For a moment Scamp supposed Peda was mystically appraising the item, as he had the chest. Then when he saw Peda's hand shaking and sweat on his forehead, Scamp realized Peda hadn't decided not to touch the globe. He couldn't touch it.

"Put it back in the chest," Peda said gravely. Scamp quickly obeyed. He stared at his hands, wondering why he'd been allowed to touch the thing, and if it would somehow hurt him for it.

Peda took in a deep breath and removed the tablet from the chest. It was small and square, with one face pitch black and the other chalky white. The pictures on its surface—it didn't look like any type of writing Scamp had ever seen—were squarish and ugly and huge, as if written by a giant's hand. Looking at the markings, part of Scamp longed to know what they meant but another was very glad he didn't.

Peda studied the writing silently. The firelight turned his eyes black.

"Is this writing?" Dannika asked. "I don't recognize it. Do you, Shal'het?"

Peda didn't answer.

Mather examined the tablet. "Strange. Are these two kinds of stone? I don't see a seam between the layers—"

Peda abruptly pulled the tablet away from Mather's gaze and put it back in the chest. Then he slammed the lid shut. A quick twist of his thumb and the lock was secured once more.

He turned on the trio. "Go, right now, and never speak of this chest again. Do not mention it to your parents or friends, not even to each other. It does not exist!" His stare was so stern it made Scamp's belly turn to water that puddled in his shoes. "Swear it on Majere's ever-watching eyes."

Dannika appeared stunned by the demand. "I . . . I swear by Majere."

Scamp and Mather shared a confused look, but each nodded his agreement. With that Peda ushered them out of the house. As Scamp was pushed out the doorway he tried to snatch one last look at the chest. Peda's body blocked his view.

When the three were outside, Peda said, "Nothing you have seen this night is real. It is less than a dream that you will forget. You have all sworn. Remember." With that, he shut the door.

Scamp, Mather, and Dannika walked home in silence. Even Scamp had sense enough to know that it was a good thing Peda was keeping the chest—the safe thing. Still, he couldn't help feeling deep down inside that he'd abandoned the greatest adventure he would ever have.

CHAPTER 5

It was well past midnight when Patima and her "comrades" found the hovel on the outskirts of town. Two of her companions were warriors, armored in colored scales and with swords drawn—dragonslayers from Tarsis. Murderers.

The third, small and weak-looking in contrast to the warriors' stature, was robed in soft black velvet trimmed in silver. The runes in the trim marked him as a Black Robe, a wizard of Nuitari. All wizards drew their power from one of Krynn's three moons: Solinari empowered white magic of good and protection, and red Lunitari's power enforced balance. Nuitari's magic was as black as the hole the moon cut in the sky. This black magic made this man more dangerous than both warriors combined.

How she hated them all. But she needed them.

Reminding herself of this, she considered her own human form like an ill-fitting gown. As a woman, she looked mature, but too smooth skinned to be called old.

She wore no armor, carried no weapons, and was adorned in no magical garb. Even in this paltry form she needed no such baubles for protection. Her hair was tarnished, a strange bronze color that repelled light. Her eyes were the same color and glowed in the dimness, so whenever she looked at the Tarsians, the men grew unsettled. This always gave her a certain amount of pleasure.

She stared at the Black Robe, who unfortunately never seemed disturbed by her presence. "You are certain the chest is here?" she asked.

He laid a finger against his bloodless lips in an impertinent gesture for silence. "You will see."

Irritated but trying not to show it, Patima opened the shack's door and entered. The others followed behind her. Inside they found a smallish, hard-looking man with pointed ears and wearing homespun garb. A bag slung over his shoulder showed he had been in the process of preparing to flee, and there was no question why: in his arms he held the chest.

The warriors spread out, blocking the hermit's escape. Patima stood in the center of the room, commanding, with the wizard behind her, his eyes glittering and eager to cast a spell. The hermit let them take their positions without moving. He didn't even look afraid. To the contrary, he looked resigned, almost peaceful.

As Patima watched, the hermit raised the chest above

his head. "Majere," he prayed aloud, "I place this chest into your trust, as I do the life of your servant."

Then he breathed onto the chest, and with a magic Patima had not seen for hundreds of years, breathed not air, but fire. The flames shot from his lips to cover the mahogany, drowning it in a white blaze that did not touch his hands. The fire raged for a moment, blinding, then was gone. The chest was gone as well, without even ash left behind.

The warriors and the mage gasped. One of the fighters nearly dropped his sword in dismay. "He destroyed it? But he . . . that's not possible!"

"It's gone," the Black Robe whispered. All animation left his sallow face, making it corpselike. Then the blank expression twisted into rage. Lifting his hands, which were clenched into claws as if to dig out the hermit's eyes, he began to chant.

Patima laid a hand on the wizard's shoulder, disrupting his casting. "There is no need. No man can destroy the contents of that chest." She looked at Peda knowingly. "Certainly not a lowly monk."

"But you cannot find it, so either way it is lost to you," Peda said.

The warriors slowly advanced on him, swords extended. The wizard kept a hand in the pouch at his side, ready to grab the strange and exotic items that would fuel his deadly magic. Patima simply stood, staring at the unflappable hermit with her hard, burnished eyes. Like the wizard, her gaze had no effect upon this man.

"You have taken what does not belong to you, servant of Majere," she said. "The chest and its contents are our lawful property. Return them. I have no wish to harm you but I will— Paladine forgive me—I will."

The hermit smiled gently. "Even if you were not lying, I could not."

She sighed, a tired sound that dragged her shoulders low and her chin down. She felt a terrible weight crushing her, body and spirit. Yet she spoke without hesitation. "Find the chest. Deal with him as you must."

The fighters sprang forward, eager to trap the unarmed and apparently helpless man between them. The hermit did not wait to receive their attack, however. Moving far more rapidly than the heavily armed men, he darted toward the slayer on the right, who had his sword raised over his head for a vicious chop. The monk easily stepped inside the great arc as the sword came down. Grabbing his attacker's wrist, the monk pulled in the same direction of the slash, yanking the armored man and flipping him over. The warrior crashed to the floor and began flailing like an upturned turtle.

The other swordsman lunged, trying to stab the hermit in the back. Quick as a snake, the monk trapped the flat of the blade between his forearm and body. A rapid spin and chop to his attacker's wrist, and Peda held the sword. The warrior turned just in time to see the hilt of the blade smash between his eyes. He crumpled like an empty suit of armor.

Ducking, just in case a bolt of something nasty came his way, the hermit turned and hurled the sword at the chanting wizard. Patima stood by and watched, almost hoping to see the evil man spitted like a pig. Unfortunately, the Black Robe realized his danger. Proving he was wise if not courageous, the wizard gave up his spell in order to dive out of the way. The small man crashed into a table and onto the floor, where he scurried behind the fallen table. The blade was buried in the door.

Seeing one of the Tarsians rising, the monk prepared to chop his throat and put him down for good. Judging she had stood by long enough, Patima caught the hermit's wrist. He tried to twist free, but her grip was firm as bedrock.

The hermit looked at her in shock, a reaction she completely understood. As a monk of Majere, this man had spent many years training his body for unarmed combat. Not only had he strengthened muscle and toughened bone, he had harnessed the power of his mind and will. It was the strength of the soul that made his fist as dangerous as a blade, his foot as lethal as an arrow. With such power of wisdom at his disposal, raw physical strength could not hold him.

But Patima could. And as he looked into her eyes, he saw the wisdom of ages beyond his comprehension and knew why. As she met his gaze she realized that this man saw her, not in this frail human guise, but as she truly was: a titanic being with wings that blocked out the sky and a head crowned in spines of obsidian.

He saw the strength of her soul and knew he could not fight her. However, he also saw something she did not recognize, and this filled his gaze with gentle pity. This mortal half breed pitied her! It made her mind thick and hot with rage—and shame.

"Give me the chest," she ordered.

"Two questions before I answer," he said calmly.

She blinked at him. "Ask."

"First your common name, Great One."

She stared at him a long time before answering. "Mortals call me Patima."

"Second, poor Patima, how can the wisdom of ages not save you from such despair?"

She shivered, a single tremor of agony. It felt like she had been stabbed in the belly. "You've had your questions. Will you give me the chest? And do not lie that you cannot."

She still held his wrist, knowing he was well aware how easily she could break his bones. She could not help but marvel when he softly replied, "I'm sorry, I will not."

A dragonslayer, still bleeding from where the hermit had struck him between the eyes, laid his sword against the monk's throat. "Let's see how many pieces I have to cut off him before he talks," he growled.

The hermit never broke his gaze from Patima's. She could scarcely bear to meet it because of the shame she felt.

"That will not work," she said. Reluctantly, she faced the wizard, who was brushing himself off and trying to look dignified, as if he hadn't just crawled from beneath a table. "Do you have any methods that will cause a monk to speak?"

The Black Robe smirked. "That I might, mistress. However, my 'methods' might strike your soft heart as, shall we say, distasteful."

Patima looked at the monk one last time in invitation. He gently shook his head. Her sorrow and regret were drowned out by bitterness and intense hatred. Tugging on his wrist, she hurled him into a wall. He crumpled in a corner, dizzy and hurt.

Patima turned her back on him. "Do what you must."

Then she walked out of the shack, the two dragonslayers close behind, leaving the hermit hurt and alone with the wizard.

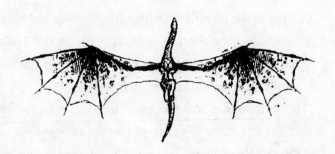

CHAPTER 6

Patima, in pitiful human form, stood outside Peda's shack, staring at the constellation of the Platinum Dragon in the midnight sky. She thought of Paladine, her creator, and how she had once loved and worshiped him and the other gods of good, and how she hated them now—because they should have known.

They should have known Takhisis, the Dark Queen, had plotted to rule the world. The legendary Huma's lance had not pierced deep enough to purge that ambition from her.

They should have known that the Dark Queen would find a way to manipulate the good dragons to keep them from resisting her as they had done in ages before, and that the metallic dragons' vulnerable eggs were in danger because of this.

They should have known that Patima's children would be taken from her and changed, twisted with vile magic into monstrous draconians.

Paladine, she thought brokenly, you should have known they'd take my babies. You should have stopped them.

Her tortured thoughts were interrupted by a scream from the hovel. It was a weak, trembling sound made by someone with no strength left.

"The Black Robe said he could get the monk to give up the chest," she said. "I don't think this will work. He's just being vicious."

One of the dragonslayers shrugged. "Maybe. So?"

The other, sitting in the dirt and trying to stop his forehead from bleeding, added, "You've heard such screams before, just as we have."

Patima couldn't deny the claim. The dragonslayers were from the razed city of Tarsis, one of the first cities destroyed in the War of the Lance. These men, and those few like them with whom she had allied herself, had watched the Red Dragonarmy destroy everything they treasured: their homes and shops, friends, even family had perished in the storm of red-scaled fury that spat fire as it passed. She knew the sitting warrior, Danton, had lost two children, a boy and a girl, neither even five years old yet.

After Takhisis lost the war, most of her evil dragons had scattered and hidden, driven apart by greed and jealously of each other. Now the Tarsian slayers hunted them one by one in revenge for their destroyed home. Patima knew it was revenge they took and not justice. They'd abandoned the pursuit of justice long ago. She did not care.

But that didn't mean it was right to hurt this monk so.

She turned, determined to march through the door and stop the torture. Before she reached the door, one of the dragonslayers asked, "Did your mate scream like this when the chromatic dragons killed him?"

She froze, trapped again by haunted dreams. She was flying—fighting and killing the monstrous kin that had taken her children. At her side was her mate, Gildagorian, strong and beautiful and even larger and older than she. He was her only joy now that her children were gone. And he was strong, so strong, too powerful to ever be harmed—or so it had seemed.

She'd grown distracted in battle with a vicious Green and its rider. Dizzy and in pain from the Green's poisonous breath, she left her mate's flank. After a chase she finally struck the dragon and rider from the air with her deadly lightning breath. Realizing she'd left Gildagorian, she wheeled about in the sky, searching for him. Her only glimpse was a flicker of bronze covered in blue, green, and red scales. It must have taken nearly a dozen of the chromatics to overpower him, and as she watched, they plummeted to the earth in a writhing ball.

She heard her mate's dying screams in the cries of the monk. Without realizing why, only knowing that she could not sit by and let this happen again, she ran to the shack. She shattered the locked door with one hand, and a blast of heat struck her.

The building was on fire. Covering her face in her arms, she pressed through the blaze. The fire licked eagerly at her weak human flesh, trying to consume her. While a fire such as this was no serious danger—she was a dragon, after all, a creature of magic—moving through the blaze was agony.

Finally, she found the monk lying on the floor amid the flames. He was dead. She was too late. Knowing there was nothing she could do for the poor man, she fled the inferno.

Outside, the Black Robe was waiting with a satisfied look on his gaunt face. How she hated that pale skin, those eyes that looked at every living creature as if it were an experiment to be cut apart and studied.

The shack was now a single ball of flame.

"You killed him," she rasped, her throat raw from smoke.

"My methods can be taxing," he said calmly. "He resisted when he should not have."

The Tarsians watched the fire spread to the roof as if the burning shack were a campfire crackling pleasantly. "Should we wait?" one of the dragonslayers asked. "It may be easy to find the chest once the fire has had its way."

Patima refused to look away from the blaze. She hid both her sorrow and guilt. Such emotions meant nothing to these people. And she needed these men, evil and vile as they were, to gain justice for her lost children and slain mate. For that, no sin was too great.

"The monk was not foolish enough to hide the chest where a simple sifting of the ashes would reveal it," she said.

"Then what do you suggest, *dragon?*" one of the slayers demanded. As always, he hissed the word "dragon" as if it were a curse.

"The Black Robe can scry our next step," she said. She called him "Black Robe" because she did not know his name, and did not care to know. "We should leave before we draw undue attention."

The slayers and the wizard looked at each other and shrugged. They followed her without complaint. After all, the argument was sound. But in truth she wished to leave this place because she could not stand to see the fire and know that a body burned inside, and worst of all, to know that she had not stopped it. All that was once good in her was gone.

For revenge, so be it.

CHAPTER 7

The next morning, Dannika stood in the burned husk that was once the home of her mentor, friend, and surrogate father. All that was left of Peda's shack was a skeleton of blackened walls and bits of furniture and other items too charred to name. The girl stood in the ruins, looking around for anything that had survived.

Scamp watched his friend's search and wished there was something he could do to make her feel better. He knew there wasn't. Scenes like this were not new to him, not to any of them really. They'd all seen homes burned to open pits of ash. Worse, they'd all attended funerals like Peda's that morning, and he knew nobody could make things right again.

The villagers had watched the forest fire well into the night, wondering at its source and watching to be sure it didn't turn in the direction of the village. They'd still been watching when Scamp snuck home and into bed. When the fey glow died, they'd thought the threat had passed, that Tarban had escaped unscathed.

Then Peda's ruined shack had been discovered. No one understood how the fire could have swung all the way around the village to the west to devour poor, lone Peda while touching nothing else. But it had. Some had argued it was simply an unfortunate accident. A few others had shared darker theories about renegade dragonarmy soldiers or dark magic. What could not be disputed was the body. Peda's remains had been buried in the dusty earth as the sun rose. Scamp hadn't been able to force himself to look at what was left of the kind man's remains.

Dannika hadn't been able to look away until the final shovelful of earth was placed upon the grave. Then she ran into the forest as fast as she could go. Scamp, and Mather soon after, had followed her to the smoking shell of Peda's home.

Dannika hadn't cried all day. Now, as she held the blackened leg of a chair, Scamp saw tears on her dark cheeks.

Scamp had always been fascinated by Dannika's skin, which was the color of moist, fresh turned earth. It was a sign of her Nordmaarian heritage. Ever since he'd known her, he'd dreamed of great oceans conquered by a race of giants with skin as black as midnight. Her skin was beautiful. Now it was dull and dirty, the color of soot and ruin. Her tears cut paths that looked like scars through the grime. She cradled the broken chair leg to her stomach as if fearing it, too, would crumble to ash.

"We should do something," Scamp whispered to his older brother. "Say something, I don't know. We should help her."

Mather shook his head, though even his harsh features showed a measure of pity. "How?"

"I don't know," Scamp admitted. "But we should."

"You can't fix a lot of things that you should," Mather said. It was the type of comment that made Scamp so angry with his always-grim brother, but at that moment he had no reply.

Scamp watched Dannika wander through Peda's former home. She moved aimlessly, almost as if unaware of what she was doing. Suddenly, she ducked with a strangled cry, disappearing from view.

"Danni?" Scamp ran toward the shack. "Danni, are you—"

He found her kneeling in the soot in what had once been the shack's lone bedroom. As he watched she held an open palm over a floorboard, as Peda had the chest. She certainly felt something, because with a small cry—part surprise, part sorrow—she pulled the board loose. Inside there was a small recess untouched by the fire. From this space she pulled a few objects: a dried rose pressed flat between two sheets of paper, a rolled-up rug, and a half-burned stub of candle made of red wax with veins of gold.

Danni looked at each item as if it were a priceless treasure, but it was the candle that drew tears from her again. "Peda . . ."

Moving slowly, not wanting to intrude, Scamp approached his friend. "Were these his?"

She shook her head, making the beads in her braided hair click. "Mine. They were gifts of wisdom." She held up the dried rose, a peculiar combination of purple and red. "Sometimes the oddest flowers are the most beautiful," she whispered. Then she raised her other hand, which held the rug. "Remember that prayer puts the mind in the heavens, not the knees in the dirt."

"What about the candle?" he asked.

Dannika fought to find her voice through her tears. "A prayer candle. Its smoke is supposed to carry a last good-bye to those who have . . ." She dropped her head, unable to finish.

Scamp didn't know what to do. How did you make people feel better when they cried, especially girls? Whatever you did just seemed to make things worse. They always cried more.

Then he realized, maybe more crying wasn't always bad.

He spotted a flicker at the foot of a burned wall—an

ember. There were still a few places burning. Kneeling, he grabbed a dry twig that had fallen though the destroyed roof and carefully lit the tip.

He held it out to Dannika, smiling gently. "Why don't you say good-bye, then?"

Offering him a weak smile, she took the candle in both hands and closed her eyes. Scamp thought he saw her mouth the word "Majere." She reverently touched the candlewick to the spark.

Instead of lighting normally, the entire candle burst into radiant white flame. Suddenly the burned shack was filled with swirling winds, strong but not violent. For some reason the gusts drove away the smoke and ash in the air, leaving a sweet freshness.

I knew you would find my voice, my little shell.

"Peda!" Dannika exclaimed.

Scamp couldn't believe it, but she was right. The voice belonged to the dead hermit. Scamp watched the wind churn around them. This wasn't what he'd expected a ghost to look like.

The disembodied voice laughed. *I am no spirit, children, at least not in this world. I embark upon a new adventure of understanding with Majere to lead me.*

Dannika looked like she was trying to be happy. If so, she couldn't manage it. "Oh Shal'het, why did you go?"

Because it was my time, and we do not mourn those who

have made their mark in life and passed on.

"But . . . you left me."

Because your time has not yet come, and your great deeds are not yet done. Dannika, brave child, I did not leave the candle for our good-byes. We are parted only for a time. No, my lovely shell, I have a final charge for you. I am sorry to place such a burden on your shoulders, for despite all your wisdom and courage, you are yet young and may not be ready. But there is no choice.

The stern words had a drastic effect on her. She raised her chin proudly and squared her shoulders. "I am ready, Shal'het, for what must be."

Good. Then know that the chest you brought me is a thing of terrible power, somehow both good and evil. But it is sought by those driven mad by sorrow and hate, and they must never find it or their revenge will know no limits upon Krynn—and they will certainly kill you as they did me. To keep yourself and many others safe, you must discover the secrets it holds.

Taken aback, she asked, "But how am I—"

The wind moaned as it lost speed. It sounded like someone's breath growing faint over distance. Indeed, when Peda spoke again his words were barely audible.

I have no more time. Listen, my young friends, and heed well: Go south and east until you find the home of newborn magic that floats upon the sea. There you will learn the deeper truth. And know that your quest cannot be completed alone. Many that you meet have a destiny entwined with yours, but of these know three, for your success will be found in their hands: the messenger who is a mirror, the outcast whose curse is a blessing, and the enemy who is your greatest friend.

Something in the voice made Scamp know that the instructions were not for Dannika alone. "Peda, I don't understand? What are we—"

"Me, not 'we,' " Danni cut him off. "Now quiet! Peda, tell me—"

I am sorry but there is no more time. The wind was now so weak that the stink of smoke was there again. *My charge is yours, Dannika, but not yours alone. Remember that pride never led to greatness. May the gods watch over you, as I know they do, and may Majere's wisdom guide your way. Good-bye.*

Before either Scamp or Dannika could protest, the wind died, leaving utter stillness. A moment later the candle, still burning with white flame, exploded. A ball of fire shot into the air, leaving a trail of sparks behind. Scamp and Dannika watched in awe that turned to panic as the ball of flame hung suspended for a moment then plummeted straight toward them.

Before Scamp could even think of moving, Dannika shoved him out of the way. She dived aside herself just as the fireball crashed to the ground. Instead of spraying flame everywhere, however, the fire opened at the top almost like a bag. It quickly shrunk down to the earth and was gone.

The mahogany chest stood in the flame's place, unsinged and open.

As the two teens stared at the chest, waiting to see if it was done flying around and bursting into flame, Mather came running.

"What in the name of the gods was that?"

"A friend's last request," Dannika said. Standing up, she approached the chest. "I'll leave today."

"*We'll* leave today," Scamp corrected, jumping up.

"You're not going anywhere," Mather ordered. "And what is she talking about, 'friend's request?' "

"Peda asked us to save Krynn," Scamp said.

Mather smacked his forehead. "Scamp, not now—"

"Did you see the fire, huh?" Scamp asked. "You know, flying around spitting sparks. It turned into the chest. Or how else do you think it got here?"

"Maybe it was here the whole time, since last night," he said.

"And it didn't burn?" Scamp shook his head. "Believe what you want, Mather. Peda told us to discover its secrets. It's a quest. When a ghost tells you to do something, you do it. When you see your first ghost you'll understand."

"I told you, Scamp, there is no 'we,' " Dannika said. "Peda was my Shal'het. The charge is mine." Strutting with self-importance, or so it seemed to Scamp, she walked to the chest and reached in. She took out the stone tablet and hid it inside the rolled-up prayer rug. Then she reached for the stone globe.

Her hands stopped before they touched it.

"Didn't you hear what Peda said?" Scamp demanded. "No pride. Well, I'm offering my help and you'd better take it or the gods'll make your hair fall out or something."

"I can't touch it," she interrupted.

"You aren't going anywhere," Mather repeated.

"What?" Scamp said, dismissing his brother.

"I said I can't touch it!" Dannika repeated. "I can't touch the globe!"

The brothers looked into the chest to see her hands shaking with the effort of trying to touch the stone. She couldn't get closer than within a few fingers' width. Furious, she looked at Scamp as if it were his fault.

"You try," she told Mather.

Shrugging, he made as if to grab the globe in one strong hand. His hand stopped just as Dannika's had done. For a few moments he pushed as hard as he could, trying to touch the stone face. Eventually, gasping for breath and sweaty faced, he gave up.

"Magic!" Dannika whispered.

"Maybe," Mather said grimly. "Whatever it is, that stone isn't going anywhere, ghost or not."

Curious, Scamp reached into the chest. His finger brushed the stone globe without any resistance at all.

Grinning, he lifted it out of the chest and displayed it for the others to see. Dannika looked at him intensely. Mather looked sick.

"I guess I'm going after all," Scamp crowed.

Dannika stared at him for a long moment, but eventually nodded. Mather raked his hair back so hard Scamp thought he'd pull himself bald. For his part Scamp just grinned, knowing a great adventure had begun, and knowing that he was now a part of it.

What were adventures supposed to be like, anyway? Scamp considered the question in light of his present situation: He was sitting in the back of an old, rickety wagon, trying not to bite his tongue off from all the bumps. Dannika was wedged beside him in the small wagon bed, and no matter how he wiggled, her elbow always seemed to jab his ribs. And, naturally, Mather walked behind the cart, glaring at him so persistently Scamp knew he'd not give it up until Scamp turned belly up and agreed to go home.

Things were not going as Scamp thought they should.

To summon the spirit of exploration he'd felt when they first snuck away from Tarban, he decided he needed a knife. Yes, how could one not feel more adventuresome holding a knife?

Grabbing his knapsack, he searched through the few things he'd brought for the journey. He had food—all of an extremely chewy nature such as dried apples and smoked pork—a few articles of spare clothing, an extra water skin, the small fishing net he used in Lowfeld Creek . . . ah, there they were.

He removed a folded handkerchief and unwrapped it. Inside was a sheathed knife about as long as his hand, and the darts he'd taken from the target in Peda's yard. Looking at the weapons, he felt a swell of pride and power.

Then he glanced at the others.

Mather carried his huge bow, nearly as tall as its owner, and a quiver of arrows. As if that weren't enough, strapped to his back was the heavy chopping axe they used for firewood. While not exactly glamorous, the axe was more than effective. In Mather's thick arms, three big whacks would fell an ogre.

As for Dannika, she'd brought along the willow staff Peda had given her years ago. It was only as thick as Scamp's thumb and he'd once thought it a toy. No more. He'd seen the girl whirl that twiggy shaft so fast it blurred, and when she hit something it made a loud *whack* like a cracking whip.

Scamp looked from Mather to Dannika and tried not to feel like a tagalong. Mather could have chopped him into bits if he wanted to take the trouble. If he didn't, he could just shoot him from a league away. That didn't bother Scamp so much. When you grew up smaller than other boys, you quickly learned to admit when you were outmatched in a fight. It was a matter of survival, not pride. Knowing that your best friend could probably paddle you was different, especially when that friend was a girl.

Suddenly, holding his knife and little darts, Scamp felt quite silly.

"Put those away," Mather hissed, "before the peddler sees you."

To make better time—and to save their feet—they'd bartered a spot on the wagon of a traveling peddler leaving their village. The old grouch was leather faced and hunched and had hair that looked like those scraggly bushes where animals went to die. He had a wagon loaded with goods, and while Scamp was convinced it was all junk, there was a lot of junk. The bed was so full he and Dannika were crammed against one wall and surrounded by sacks of worn linen, chipped stone jewelry, crooked pewter candlesticks, and anything else Scamp could imagine people wouldn't really want. When Mather had offered to walk guard in exchange for letting them all hitch a ride, the peddler took one look at Mather's shoulders and told them to hop on.

Scamp glanced over his shoulder and saw the peddler staring straight ahead. "He isn't even paying attention," Scamp told his brother.

"Neither are you," Mather said.

Scamp wondered what he meant until he felt the

stone globe slipping off his knees. Scrambling to catch it, he almost stabbed his own hand. In his rush to save the globe—and trying not to sever his own fingers—he grew careless with the knife and cut hard along the side of the stone. The blade drew a line of sparks that made Dannika nearly jump from the cart. Once everything was settled, the globe in one hand and the knife in the other, Scamp looked around sheepishly.

"Um, it's all right now. I've got it," he said.

Mather snorted. "You should have dropped it. With luck it would've broken to pieces and we'd be done with this foolery."

Dannika shook her head grimly. "I doubt it. Look at the globe."

Scamp studied the stone and noticed what she meant right off: the knife hadn't even scratched the surface. The pattern on the face had shifted, however, turning sharp and jagged. It almost looked angry.

"And look at this." She pulled the stone tablet out of her prayer rug. "Give me your knife, Scamp."

When he did, she placed the tip against the center of tablet and twisted, drilling down hard. The rock didn't dimple or flake. Not a single grain of stone dislodged.

"See? Here, you try." She tossed it to Mather. He took the tablet in both hands and pulled, twisting and wrenching, trying to crack it. He fought until he was red faced. The tablet stayed undamaged. Giving up, he tossed it back to Dannika.

"There's nothing we can do to harm these things," she said, tucking the tablet back inside the prayer blanket. "Our charge is to find someone who can, or will at least protect them."

"Why?" Mather asked, not for the first time.

"Because they are evil, because someone wants to use that evil, and because I swore to Peda that we would," Dannika retorted.

"Swore that *you* would," Mather corrected. "You'll not be making any promises to ghosts for me."

"Then why don't you go back home?" Scamp demanded.

"Eagerly, so come with me."

"Tough tickles to that!"

"Scamp, I'm not going home to tell Mother and Father that you've gone to get yourself killed in some strange way, even if you deserve it."

"What makes you think that home is safe?" Dannika demanded. "It wasn't for Peda."

The brothers went silent. Scamp stared at his shoes and felt a good deal lower than that. So many exciting things were happening that he sometimes forgot someone had died. Maybe he meant to forget. After all, whenever he remembered, something inside him grew small and hard and very frightened.

Dannika glared at both of them. "Going home or going on makes no difference, we'll not be safe. Someone is looking for these. They killed Peda to find them, and they'll kill us too if we're found. Our only hope is to find someone who knows what these things are."

"You call that a hope?" Mather said. "We don't even know where we're going."

"Southeast," Scamp said helpfully.

"And why?"

"To find the newborn magic on the sea," Dannika said.

"And that, of course, means what?" Mather asked.

Dannika lifted her chin. "We'll know when the time is right."

Mather shook his head and chuckled. "Right." Suddenly the youth's expression hardened and his gaze shifted to something ahead of the wagon. Scamp noted his brother's free hand had edged closer to the quiver on his hip.

"What—" Dannika said, but before she could finish the cart lurched to a halt, nearly bucking both of them off the bed.

"Move yer bloody backside off'r the road," the peddler bellowed. He waved the driving whip with which he frequently thrashed his poor spindle-legged draft horse. "Get yerself gone, beggar, or it's the lash!"

Finally righting himself, Scamp looked ahead to see a

man blocking the cart's way. The man stood in the middle of the road, appraising them. His gray tabard was worn and soiled, and Scamp suspected the grayness was more a result of color bled away over time than an original finish. His boots had the look of being well used, as did his leather pack. Most battered of all, however, were the leather scabbard that lay on the man's left hip and the man himself. Both appeared weathered and worn to the brink of raggedness. It was difficult to say which creases were deeper and more plentiful, those on the scabbard or those on his angular face. The only orderly thing about the man was his beard, which was thick, blond, and well trimmed.

"Pardon, master merchant," the man called. "Seeing that you travel my way I should like to barter passage."

"You?" the peddler scoffed. "I got no interest in tradin' fer dirt, which is all you is. Get yerself off or I'll run you down."

The stranger did not act offended. "If you've no mind to trade then perhaps you'll accept coin?"

The peddler's look turned from disgusted to greedy. "Coin? Good copper?"

"Better. Steel." The stranger reached into the pocket of his tabard, drew something out, and with a flick of his thumb, sent it spinning to the peddler, who dropped his reins and nearly toppled from the cart trying to catch it. Peeking at the item, Scamp saw the dull wink of genuine steel.

"Good?" the stranger asked.

The peddler didn't look away from the coin when he nodded. Thumbing toward the cart bed, he said, "Get yerself in quick."

The stranger jumped up onto the driver's seat instead. The peddler stared at him as if he were a sewer rat on an inn pillow, but the stranger looked calmly back. The peddler did not demand that he move. Scamp suspected that the way the man sat with his hand resting on his blade's hilt, not threateningly but easily, as if the position was very natural, had something to do with the peddler clamping tight his cantankerous tongue.

Mather stared at the man's sword. "I don't like this."

"We were bound to meet others on the journey," Dannika said, though she didn't sound entirely easy herself. "Peda said as much, remember, and success lies in the hands of a special three."

"You think he's just a soldier looking for hire?" Scamp whispered. "Or could he be—"

"I don't know," Dannika admitted. "But I think we should be careful. Don't let him see the globe until we know more."

Scamp quickly buried the globe inside his makeshift pack. He'd barely finished when the stranger turned around.

"Greetings, children," he said. "We're to be companions for a time, so well met. My name is Anden Tillis. Where are you bound?"

Mather glared back silently. Scamp knew he was boiling about being included in the term "children."

"We're just on a bit of an adventure," Scamp said, judging the answer vague enough.

For some reason the man's knowing look made him fear that he hadn't been vague after all.

"Adventures don't come in bits, boy," Anden said. "They come in one size only—great. If you've stumbled onto a true adventure then fortune be with you because you'll need it." With a quick smile, and a strange look at Mather, he turned around as the peddler started the cart off again.

CHAPTER 9

After days with little or no news of the chest, Patima was out of patience. Unlike usual, turning back to her magnificent dragon form hadn't improved her mood. It didn't matter what she did. Even flying couldn't shift her mind from the knowledge of what she was doing—and it looked like it all might come to nothing.

In her frustration her hate grew.

She hated the chromatic dragons and all servants of Takhisis, and hourly swore painful retribution for her slaughtered mate and kidnapped children.

She hated the Tarsian dragonslayers for their incompetence and cruelty, for she could no longer deny that they had crossed completely into the pursuit of evil.

She hated herself for allying with them and doing as they did, and not having the courage to stop herself.

But one above all she grew to hate most, and when they met in a forest clearing to discuss what to do next, she decided to show her displeasure.

Five Tarsians were already in the clearing when the Black Robe sauntered out of the tree line. Despite his continued futility in scrying the lost chest, he always kept that infuriating look of superiority on his face—a look he dared maintain even when he looked at her, the most magnificent breed in creation. When she saw that same pompous expression again now, in her foul mood, she met it with a blast of lightning.

The bolt shot from her mouth and left the familiar tingle throughout her body. She watched eagerly as it streaked toward the frail, hated mage. She reveled in the thought that it might hit him and leave nothing but ash. It would be a good thing, and it had been a long time since she had done anything good.

But all too soon, the bolt hit the ground, blasting clumps of soil and sod into the air. When the dirt and smoke cleared the mage was there, waving his hands before his face.

"Forgive me for saying so, Great One," he mocked, "but that wasn't entirely constructive."

"Perhaps not, but it was refreshing," Patima said. What a relief it was to speak with the power of a dragon's voice, a voice that shook the earth. "You try my patience too long, wizard. Provoke me again, for I've been known to miss on occasion. What news of the chest?"

"I found it," he answered. He left their stunned silence intact for a moment before adding, "Empty."

Patima felt that hollow place inside her howl at the prospect of revenge lost. Another part of her, however, was almost glad.

"Then our business is concluded," she said. She glared at the dragonslayers, who viciously stared back, then at the Black Robe. "Despite your failures, I will allow you all to live. So leave. I'll not be so generous if you ever intrude upon me again."

To accent this point she lashed her tail against a tree, or more accurately, through it. The strong cedar exploded into a hail of slivers and the trunk toppled through the canopy with a ponderous groan. Its landing shook the earth.

Patima turned to leave.

"Not so hasty, Great One," the Black Robe said. "I have another way of finding our prize, if it is worth it to you."

Patima froze. "How?"

Instead of answering, the Black Robe began to chant. He spoke in a whisper so soft that the dragon could not completely make out his words, but even so, she thought they were wrong. Patima, like all dragonkind, was magical. The mystical elements of creation—fire, water, earth, and air—made up her muscle, scale, and bone. As such, magic was her birthright. Yet she somehow did not know what kind of magic the Black Robe summoned.

This made her trust him even less. She was cautious

as she waited, barely breathing, to see the results of the spell.

As he cast the spell the wizard pulled a square of red cloth from his robes. He held the cloth with one hand, and when he finally finished chanting, gently blew on the square.

A sharp, growling wind filled the clearing, and in the wind could be heard the triumphant shriek of a wordless voice.

"What have you summoned?" Patima demanded.

In answer, the Black Robe pointed to a distortion in the air. It was small and barely visible, like a spot where the wind could actually be seen. Black dots swirled and churned in the spot. As they stood by and watched, the motes thickened. More gathered from every direction, and Patima finally realized what the spots were—insects.

The blur of specks in the air congealed into a swarm. Its buzz was ugly and loud and made Patima feel like needle-tipped feet were crawling along her bones. The sensation only grew more powerful as the swarm, nearly the size of a horse, began to take shape.

Four tendrils of roped-together insects descended to the ground like legs. The bulk of the swarm condensed into one great ball of bug on bug, a body. Last, a bulge of milling insects sprouted from the front of the mass and split in two, forming a gaping maw. The creature's surface, all beating wings and lashing legs, stilled and smoothed. Finally, two pits opened in the swarm-thing's head. Inside, two bits of hellish red shone with intelligence, malice, and rage.

A great dog stood before them, only this canine had hair and flesh and tooth all made of live, squirming insects.

The dragonslayers, both harsh, brutal men, edged back in disgust. "What is that thing?" one asked, his voice cracking.

"A ghovar," Patima growled in loathing.

"Your knowledge of planar ways is impressive, Great One," the Black Robe said. He looked at his summoned monstrosity with pride. "Spirits from the edge of the Abyss, where the plane of shadow intrudes. They are formless, and cursed to remain so by the gods at the founding of Krynn. If you give them hosts, however"—he gestured to the swarm dog's milling insects—"then they will take any form you wish."

"We need no such perversion," Patima said.

The Black Robe arched one brow. "Really? Then perhaps you have a means of tracking those who have taken the contents of the chest? I do not . . . beyond the ghovar."

Patima had no alternative, and it made her seethe.

"As I thought." Turning to the swarm beast, he ordered, "Follow the stink of ash and it will lead you to a shack. There you will find the scent of our prey. Follow it. When you find who you're looking for, do not harm anything they

80

carry. Whoever you find, though,"—he glanced at Patima, smirking—"with them, you may do as you wish."

The ghovar opened its mouth, but instead of a howl, a loathsome din of clicking emerged. Then, running just like the beast it impersonated, it darted into the forest. Just before it disappeared into the tree line it ran straight into a bush. Rather than go around, it collided with the plant. The swarm dog burst into a haze of furious buzzing pests that engulfed the bush. A moment later, the swarm congealed once more into the form of a dog and continued on its way.

Patima watched it disappear into the forest shadows, though she could still hear the horrid clicking it made as it moved. She felt terribly uneasy, sitting there watching such a demon freed into the world. When she looked at the bush the swarm had enveloped, her unease grew.

The bush was practically gone. All leaves and even the bark had vanished, utterly ravaged by the swarm. The abused twigs that remained could only be called a skeleton, and made a grim impression of what would happen when the creature caught up to whoever had taken what was in the chest.

CHAPTER 10

Scamp sat in the dirt, pondering his backside, which was bruised and raw from four days in the back of the cart. Tomorrow, he determined, he would walk. Some things were far worse than sore feet.

It was night and the little group was huddled around a fire. They had already eaten their meager rations for the night. The peddler had a lot of food, but he never shared. The others were left with the mundane trail fare they brought with them. The food didn't bother Scamp—though it was terribly boring—but Mather complained constantly of being hungry.

The peddler kept to himself, and the others left him that way. Every evening when they stopped he would gobble down his meal—along with an equal measure of spirits— then roll into a lump and start to snore. He usually slept by the horse—to keep it from being stolen, he said. He looked at Scamp when he said it, which seemed awfully rude. But that was the best way to describe the fellow—very awful and very rude. Scamp did not miss his presence at all at the fire.

Anden was a different story. Over the four days the stranger had traveled with them, the man had become an exciting mystery. He was full of tales of travel beyond the ends of the world, or so it seemed to Scamp, who knew nothing but fables about lands other than Abanasinia. Anden, it seemed, had visited all those strange places. He passed the days in the cart by telling of marching through Icereach with melted blubber on his cheeks, and sailing the Blood Sea to hunt down marauding minotaur pirates. Yet in all these tales of travel, somehow he never seemed to mention where he came from or where he was heading now.

That night, Anden had decided not to tell any stories. He simply sat staring into the fire. His expression made Scamp wonder what he saw in the flames, and why it worried him so.

Scamp shifted position, trying to sit in a way that hurt less. Nothing worked. So to distract himself, he turned his thoughts to a second mystery.

He took his pack, opened the top, and shifted the contents until he could see the stone globe. As always, its face was blotchy, covered by strange patterns that looked like swirling clouds.

Even more peculiar, the patterns moved.

When he tried to tell Dannika and his brother this,

they refused to believe him. Mather always said it looked like it moved because Scamp never sat still. Invariably, this was followed with a command to leave the globe alone. It was evil, Mather said. Dannika didn't disagree, at least not enough to argue.

But Scamp couldn't help but wonder. Was the globe evil? Peda had told them that it could be, but didn't that mean it could be good as well? In that way it didn't sound different from any person. And had the kindly hermit really been murdered because of these things? That thought always frightened him and made him feel bitter and angry toward the item he kept in his pack.

But for some reason the anger never stayed.

He studied the globe by the firelight and wondered why. Why, despite all the evidence to the contrary, did he so much want to know that the globe was really good? In the tinted light the swirls on the stone face looked like veins. The orb looked more like a living organ than a stone. He could almost see blood flowing, swirling in small rivulets.

But . . . it was moving! Not just the pattern on the exterior, but something beneath. He could see it as a shadow moving beneath the swirl. Something was inside.

"Psst! Danni!" he whispered.

She didn't look away from the fire. "Yeah."

The globe was now jumping in his hands. Then the

surface pressed upward, distended by something inside. He didn't know how stone could flex, but it did.

"Danni, Mather, look quick!" he begged.

"What are you hissing at?" Mather asked.

"It's alive!"

Mather rolled his eyes, then rolled over. "Won't you ever be tired enough not to be silly? Go to sleep."

Dannika and Anden still stared at the fire.

Before Scamp could speak another word, there was a quiet crack and a fracture appeared on the stone. Scamp stared at the fault, and his stomach started churning.

Oh no, Scamp thought, I broke it! Nobody else can even touch the thing and I crack it right down the middle.

The crack grew longer and wider until the globe split in half. To his shock, it was only an outer covering of shale that fell away, leaving behind another sphere, this one pocked and dimpled and gleaming wetly in the firelight. It was hard to tell, but he thought it was green.

It took him a moment to recognize the item. An egg. A big green egg in a chest he had taken off the body of a really big, green dragon.

"Oh, no."

Mather sat bolt upright and Dannika looked away from the fire. Even Anden abandoned his private thoughts to consider Scamp.

"What did you do now?" Mather demanded.

Scamp was speechless as he watched the egg crack open. A small fragment of shell fell away, revealing a tiny head so glossy green it was almost black. A pair of overlarge eyes met his gaze. Then the head slowly extended from the shell and out of the pack, propelled by a long neck. The wyrmling dragon flared the small ridge on the back of its neck, opened its mouth . . .

And cooed.

"Whoa!" Mather scrambled away on his hands and knees. In his haste, his foot snagged on a fallen log and he plunged face first into the dirt.

Dannika fled as well, rolling behind a bristling pine. Even Anden leaped to his feet, grabbing his sword hilt, though he did not pull it free of the scabbard.

Scamp simply looked at the tiny dragon, who stared right back. He turned its small head this way and that, like an owl. Scamp understood. Everything the dragon was seeing was new and exciting. And he was the very first thing the dragon had ever seen, which made him new and exciting. Scamp liked that.

"Hello, baby," he said.

The wyrmling blinked, real eyelids, not those fake clear ones Scamp had noticed on lizards. It cooed again.

"I'm keeping him," Scamp vowed then and there. "I think I'll call him Pug."

"But . . . it's a dragon!" Dannika stammered.

"A green dragon," Mather said. He spit, trying to get the taste of dirt out of his mouth. "Green dragons are evil, Scamp."

Scamp extended his finger toward the wyrmling, figuring a single finger bitten off would be better than losing an entire hand. The baby just stared as Scamp wiggled the digit back and forth. Eventually, Scamp tickled under the dragon's long neck and Pug burbled and murmured pleasantly. The wyrmling stretched his neck for more attention.

"Oh yeah, he looks absolutely wicked," Scamp said.

"How do you know it's a he?" Dannika said, easing out from behind her tree.

"Of course he's a he," Scamp said patiently. "He's a dragon. Dragons don't come in shes."

"They do too!" she retorted.

"Whoever heard of a girl dragon?" Scamp laughed and tickled Pug again. "A girl dragon!"

"If there are no girl dragons then where did the egg come from?" She folded her arms and looked at him archly.

"That old drunk Wendell the Wondrous—you know, the one who smelled like dwarven spirits and feet—he used to pull eggs out of his hat all the time," Scamp pointed out. "If he could do that, you think a dragon would have a problem magicking up eggs too?"

"Dragons are male and female as are all the gods' creations," Anden said, staring at the wyrmling intensely. "All are forces to be reckoned with in this world. And Greens an evil nearly beyond all others—just ask the Silvanesti."

Scamp stared at Pug, troubled. He had heard the stories of Silvanesti, the ancient elf homeland twisted into a nightmare because of a single green dragon, Cyan Bloodbane. He knew green dragons were terrible, evil creatures. Even among the chromatic dragons they were infamous for their viciousness. What Anden and Mather said was true—there had never been a green dragon that was anything but pure evil.

But as he looked at Pug, listened to the little dragon jabber and hiss, and saw the innocent curiosity in his eyes, Scamp knew he was not evil. Not yet. Then and there he promised that the wyrmling would never be evil.

Scamp gently picked Pug up in his arms. His face soured at the dragon's touch—the wyrmling was slick with mucus from the egg membrane. It was like holding something covered in pork fat. However, as he held him at arm's length, Pug's head dashed forward and licked his nose.

Maybe he didn't feel so yucky after all.

"What do you think you're doing?" Mather demanded.

88

"I'm going to teach him to be good," Scamp answered.

"How's that when you've never tried it yourself?" Dannika quipped.

Ignoring her, he asked, "Could you bring over a canteen please? He's all sticky."

She reluctantly did as he asked, holding the canteen out to him with her arm fully extended so she didn't have to draw too close.

Scamp dumped the water over Pug's head, which he seemed to enjoy. He shivered and shook, moving his head to keep it in the fullest rush of the water. As the slime washed away, a pair of tiny wings lifted from his back and began to flap weakly.

"I'm sorry Scamp, but that's enough." Mather advanced on his little brother and the wyrmling, reaching behind his back for the heavy axe.

Scamp edged away. "What are you doing?"

"We have to kill it," Mather explained. "It's evil, just like Anden said. If we wait it will turn on us. It has to be done now."

"No!" Scamp hugged the baby, who wrapped his tiny wings around the boy, sharing the embrace.

"There's no choice." Mather held the axe in one strong hand as he reached for the baby dragon. Dannika and Anden looked on sad faced, but neither did anything.

Scamp turned, protecting Pug with his body. He

prepared to run when Mather grabbed his shoulder and hauled him back.

"I said enough, Scamp!"

"Let me go!" Scamp fought to free himself. He cradled the baby in his arms, trying to hide him. "You can't have him!"

"I said give me the—"

Seeing Scamp's struggles, Pug's demeanor changed. No longer cooing pleasantly or resting his head on Scamp's shoulder, he stiffened and started to hiss. The small fin on his neck and back bristled. Then, as Mather tried once more to rip the baby from his brother, the wyrmling's head shot forward like a striking snake's.

A puff of yellow-green vapor hit Mather straight in the face.

Mather stumbled back, blinking red, watering eyes. Scamp watched, terrified of what would then happen. For a moment Mather just stood there, shaking. Then, holding his stomach, he ran into the bushes and threw up.

After a few more heaves Scamp realized that his brother wasn't about to die. He was only sick. Fine then, he deserved it.

"Good job, Pug." Scamp patted the wyrmling's head.

Then, just for fun, he gulped air and offered a belch of his own.

The dragon answered with another puff.

So they started taking turns, Scamp burping air and the wyrmling burping wisps of gas.

Dannika turned away. "That's disgusting."

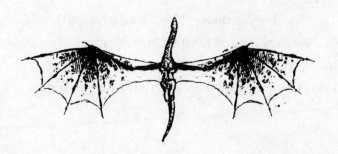

CHAPTER 11

Pug's playful burping was soft, but Scamp belched like a dwarf. It wasn't surprising that the peddler snorted and woke.

"Whatsh dat?" he mumbled. Groaning and cussing, he tottered to his knees and peered around the fire bleary eyed. Then he spotted the wyrmling.

Screaming a shrill, drunken gurgle, he hid behind his ratty blanket. "What ish that disgushting thing?"

"He's my new pet, and he's cleaner than you. He just had a bath," Scamp said, hoping the filthy man would take a hint. "Go back to sleep."

The blanket shivered. "Kill it!"

Scamp looked at Mather, who was still green faced, and grinned. "No chance, we've already covered that."

The peddler peeked over the blanket. "I shaid kill it, you brat!"

"And I said no, you thistle-brained glow nose!" As soon as he finished the insult, Scamp regretted it.

He'd gone too far, especially with that "glow nose" bit. Not that the peddler didn't deserve it. He was always liquored up and surly, and his nose was red as a cherry. But few things would make a drunk madder than calling him one, and mad drunks were one of the worst sorts of men.

The peddler dropped the blanket. His bloodshot eyes were so wide they showed white rims. His ugly scowl made him look more goblin than human.

He snatched the driver's whip off the dirt.

"I'sh gonna break that scaly lizardsh neck," the peddler said. "Then I'sh gonna whip your tongue clean, whelp."

Quickly the peddler was on his feet, blundering forward in a drunken charge.

Scamp knew he could never run fast enough to escape without abandoning Pug. Sheltering the little dragon in his arms, he looked around for help.

Unfortunately, Dannika had moved as far from their little belching contest as possible to the other side of the fire. Anden was closer, but for some reason he wasn't watching the peddler or Scamp at all—his attention was staunchly focused on Mather. His face was intense, almost excited, as if he had been waiting for this to happen and was content to watch the results.

The only one near enough to help was Mather. Scamp's older brother was still red eyed and sallow faced, and clearly still dizzy from the wyrmling's breath. But as the peddler started his charge, Mather stood as well, grabbing his axe. He took a step toward Scamp.

But then the brothers' eyes met and Mather paused.

Scamp's gaze pleaded with his older brother. It lasted only a moment, and in that moment Mather could not—or would not—move.

Then the peddler was on top of Scamp and all the boy could do was throw himself to the ground and cover Pug with his body. He hid his face to protect it and closed his eyes.

It felt as if someone stuck a hot needle into his back and dragged it from his shoulder to his hip. Immediately everything grew black and fuzzy, but around the edges of his vision was swirling red pain. A sickening crack sounded and Scamp realized it was the sound of the whip meeting his skin. Someone screamed.

It took him a moment to realize it was him.

"Stop it! Stop it . . ."

Moments or hours later, he couldn't tell, the blackness parted enough for him to make out shapes: The first, wide and lumpy and covered in dirt, was the peddler. The second, a moving shadow with a willow staff that hummed as it cut the air, was Dannika.

She was above him, lashing the peddler with her staff and shouting at him. It was only then that Scamp realized the man had stopped beating him. She's protecting me, he realized. That means I must not be dead after all.

The peddler stumbled back as Dannika's staff drew welts from his legs to his head. Scamp couldn't even see the wood beyond an ocher blur, yet somehow the peddler managed to trap the staff beneath an arm. Scowling viciously, he raised the whip to hit Dannika.

A sword point beneath his chin made him freeze.

Anden held the blade in a steady hand, his face grim and thoroughly disappointed. What was strange was that he still did not look at the purple-faced peddler, but at Mather. Scamp's brother had not moved the entire time.

Anden's expression made clear that whatever he'd expected from Mather, the youth had completely failed. Shaking his head, Anden looked away from Mather, dismissing him.

Anden's gaze was no softer when it locked onto the peddler. "It's been a long time since I've felt anger, real want-to-hurt-someone anger. I didn't miss it. I even thought I was done with it, that nothing could make me truly furious again. I was wrong." He leaned near the peddler. "Drunks who beat children make me very, very angry."

The peddler started crying. "Pleash, sir, I'm jush a working man! You don't need to cut me!"

"The question isn't do I need to," Anden said, "it's do I want to."

95

The peddler was shivering so violently, Anden withdrew his blade from the man's hairy neck so the peddler wouldn't cut his own throat with his trembling.

"Do you want to?" the peddler squeaked.

"Very much."

The filthy man looked ready to faint.

"But I won't," Anden finished, "as long as you take your junk and leave, right now."

The peddler nodded so fervently his teeth chattered. Never shifting his gaze from the sword, he scurried back to his bedroll. He hurled it carelessly into the back of the wagon and started harnessing his draft horse before the poor animal was fully awake. When it didn't respond as quickly as he wanted, he kicked it.

"And if you flog that poor beast one time this night," Anden said, "I'll track you down, take that whip, and make sure you can never peddle through these parts again. Understand?"

The peddler hurled the whip as far into the woods as he could in answer. Hopping onto his cart, he cracked the reins and didn't stop cracking them. Soon there was nothing left of the vicious old peddler but the distant creak of the cart and the sour stink of old wine.

CHAPTER 12

Scamp lay on his stomach near the fire, trying not to whimper as Dannika gently washed his cut back. At least, she said she was being gentle. To Scamp, it felt as if a rake were dragging over the gash.

What hurt even worse was the knowledge that Mather had stood and watched as he was beaten.

"There," Dannika said gently. "At least it's clean. We need something to bind the cut though. I suppose I could cut up a blouse or—"

Anden drew a roll of dressing cloth out of his pack. "Bind him from shoulder to hip," he instructed. "Not too tight. It'll draw once the wound seeps."

She took the bandaging with a grateful nod and carefully started wrapping the wound by firelight. Every touch of the cloth felt like hemp grating on Scamp's torn skin, and he had to clamp his jaw not to whimper. Even then, his eyes watered.

"That was a foolish thing to do, boy," Anden said.

"Almost as foolish as it was brave."

Scamp looked at Pug, who sat by his head nuzzling his neck. He cradled the wyrmling in his arm protectively. "He's just a baby. Someone needed to protect him."

He glanced at Mather, who was sitting away from everyone, staring at the ground.

"Foolish, as I said," Anden repeated. "But stupid bravery is always better than cowardice."

He looked straight at Mather, who did not flinch. His face was haggard and harsh in the firelight.

"There," Dannika said with satisfaction. She tugged on her bandaging to ensure it was secure. "How does that feel?"

"Fine," Scamp lied.

Wincing, he sat up. The wyrmling jumped between his legs and curled up. Pug made a strange hissing kind of purr as he rested his head on Scamp's thigh.

"I think it's time you told me where you found the chest," Anden said.

Scamp was glad he was sitting, because if he'd been standing up his legs would have dropped him. He saw the same shock in Dannika's dark eyes. Even Mather looked up.

"What?" Scamp asked, trying to buy time. It was only now, with Anden towering over him, that Scamp realized how large and powerful looking the man was.

Anden eyed him knowingly. "The chest. Mahogany with iron ribbing, as wide as my shoulders. It held an item of great importance—and a single dragon egg." He looked at the wyrmling, who was sleeping peacefully. "I've been hunting it and it just so happens I find you three with your own freshly hatched dragon. You don't ask me to believe that this is simply coincidence, do you?"

Scamp swallowed. "Why do you want it?"

"A better question," Anden said grimly, "is what I'm willing to do to get it."

Dannika glared at him. "Is that a threat?"

"Only if it needs to be," he said. "Tell me about the chest."

Dannika leaned near Scamp, who whispered, "What do we do? I don't suppose you could, you know, knock him out with an elven neck pinch or something?"

"Maybe, but I doubt it," she admitted. "He looks like he knows how to use that sword."

"So what do we say?"

"As little as possible."

She met his gaze and he was struck by the concern he saw. Dannika, he had learned, knew things about people sometimes. He didn't know how it worked, but it was as if she could look at them and see inside somehow. She could tell you what people were feeling sometimes, even if they didn't show it on their face. She could tell when people lied and if they were trustworthy. Most of all, she could tell when someone meant to do bad things.

"Do you think he's evil?" Scamp whispered.

Her face pursed quizzically. "No. It's just . . . he's hiding something. I don't know what, but I know he is."

Anden watched their whispered conversation patiently. "I don't mean to interrupt but there is not a lot of time." His expression hardened. "You have no idea what is at stake. Now, where did you find the chest?"

"Outside our village," Scamp admitted. "There was a dead dragon, a green one. It smashed the Bristling Briar to kindling, so it must have fallen from the sky. And there was another dragon, a huge Bronze, with men on its back, soldiers with armor that were all these different colors."

Anden's expression was very severe. "And the chest? Did they take the chest?"

Scamp shook his head. "They didn't find it. I did."

"And what was inside?"

Scamp wondered if he dared lie. He hadn't always been absolutely honest in his life, so he'd had some practice *stretching* the truth. But he'd never fudged anything knowing that if he was caught in the lie he might be stabbed through the middle with a sword.

Rigidly controlling his tone, he said, "Nothing. The chest was broken. I think the dragon dropped it when it died. I found the egg outside. It must have rolled away during the fall."

Anden crouched. His expression was hard enough to sharpen steel. "What else did you find?"

"Nothing." Under that gaze, it felt like Scamp had to pull the word from somewhere around his toes.

"Nothing," Anden repeated. "Are you sure?"

Scamp nodded.

Dannika supported him, adding, "We didn't even know it was an egg. It looked like a rock. You saw it, all covered in stone like that."

"Then what were you doing with it?" Anden asked.

"That's a secret," Dannika replied.

"Share it with me," he said.

"I can't. I won't. It was a promise."

"Some promises are worth keeping." His hand shifted ever so slightly toward his sword hilt. "Be sure this is one of them."

"It is," she said firmly. "Even if you draw that sword and stab it right through my chest, it is."

Scamp was startled by the passion in his friend's response. He thought she actually meant it.

Anden appeared impressed as well, at least enough to drop his hand from his weapon. "You're sure these soldiers and the dragon didn't find the chest before you?"

Scamp nodded. "They didn't get there until after I

found the egg. And I don't think they could have found anything afterward anyway because of the fire."

"Fire?" Anden asked.

"Yes," Dannika said. "Whatever it is you're looking for was probably destroyed. It's probably just ashes now."

Anden looked at them both thoughtfully. Scamp kept an innocent look on his face, despite all the worries ricocheting around inside him. Dannika stared back just as harshly as the older man.

Finally, Anden whispered, "All great lies are partly truth, so where does the truth end? You aren't telling me everything."

"Then that makes us even," Dannika said. "We both have our secrets—like, why are you so interested in Mather?"

Scamp looked at his brother, who had been sitting by the fire without moving. When he heard his name, however, Mather's head lifted and the first hint of genuine expression touched his handsome features.

Anden looked at him coldly. "The girl is right, more's the pity. I was told to watch you."

Mather straightened. "By whom?"

"Someone who thought more of you than he should," Anden replied. He turned his back on Mather.

"Where did you find the chest?" he asked Scamp.

"Outside Tarban," Scamp said, eager to see the man

leave. "Four days along the road and west, past the fork to Gateway. Look for a clearing east of town." He was a bit worried about guiding the man home, but he didn't think Anden would hurt anyone. After a moment Scamp added the bald-faced lie, "I hope you find what you're looking for."

"You should," the man replied gravely. "You have no idea what will happen if others find it first."

With that he walked away. He grabbed his worn pack, hitched it over his shoulder, and started for the woods. Suddenly he stopped. Scamp tried to see what had stopped him. He noticed nothing.

Except after a moment, he thought there was a tint of strange white light hidden by Anden's broad-shouldered body. For the life of him Scamp couldn't figure out where the light could be coming from. Then it was gone.

Anden turned around, a bitter but resigned expression on his face. "It seems that everyone gets second chances, whether or not they deserve them." He looked at Mather. "I'm to give you a gift."

"What gift?" Mather asked.

Anden reached beneath his loose tabard. Scamp spotted a glittering shirt of steel rings beneath the garment—fine chain mail. But something else lay atop the armor. It shined as well, brighter even than the steel, and looked about the size of a fist. He could just make out three points. Anden withdrew his hand, covering his chest before Scamp could make out more.

Anden extended an item to Mather, who stared at it without moving.

"Some gifts may only be offered once," Anden warned.

Mather took the item. Holding it in both hands, he examined it. His face scrunched in confusion. Peeking over his brother's shoulder, Scamp appraised the item. It was a small piece of rusted, dented metal with a dingy chain. The rust was so thick it was impossible to tell what kind of metal it hid. While the object looked roughly triangular, the tips and edges were furred with rust, making it impossible to tell for sure.

Mather looked from the item to Anden, clearly wondering what he was supposed to do or say. "What is it?" he finally asked.

Anden shook his head, a profound look of disappointment on his face. "I doubt you'll ever know, young man."

Mather snorted. Then he looked at Scamp. Being that close to his brother reminded Scamp of the cut on his back and how it got there. He walked away.

Mather stared at the ground again. He considered the rusted chunk of metal for a moment before tossing it to the dirt. "Thanks," he murmured.

Anden glowered at him. "If someone handed you the

sun, you wouldn't know what to do with it. Very well, I should at least leave you one gift you understand." He drew his sword.

Mather jumped up. He stood unarmed before Anden, who held his blade extended, eyeing Mather darkly.

Then, spinning the blade in his hand, Anden thrust it deep into the soil.

"Maybe this will persuade you to fight when others need you," he said.

With that, he walked away. Soon he reached the edge of the firelight and became a shadow in the gloom.

"Wait!" Dannika called.

The silhouette paused.

"We guided you. Now you can return the favor."

"If I can."

"We were told to find a home of newborn magic that floats upon the sea," she said. "Have you seen such a place?"

There was no sound from the darkness for a long time. "When you come to the fork to New Ports and Digfel, head east through the Dire Wood. Follow the coast. You'll find what you seek. Only pray that you are not sought in turn."

With that, he was gone.

CHAPTER 13

The next day they rose at dawn and started walking. They followed the road for as long as they could. When they reached the New Ports/Digfel fork they continued east, trusting that Anden would not lead them astray, though Scamp couldn't quite say why.

It was perhaps the most awkward day of Scamp's life. He and his brother had never been close, not the way many siblings were. They weren't confidants or conspirators, not even similar really. In a way they were more cohabitants in the same house than blood relations. But Scamp had never questioned his brother's presence in his life. Whatever he felt about it, Mather was always there.

For as long as he could remember, Scamp knew that his brother was somehow out of reach. Mather was always bigger and better. Scamp sometimes thought this was why his brother looked down on him. He couldn't help it. When your life is big and important you can't help but look down on those who aren't. Scamp resented it sometimes, but he understood—that was who his brother was and it would never change.

Last night everything changed.

Mather was no longer larger than life. He no longer had heroic proportions, was no longer bigger and better than anything Scamp would ever be. The change was clear in his posture as he walked—head down, shoulders slumped, eyes dull and unfocused. For the first time Scamp had ever seen, his older brother looked uncertain of where he was, what he was doing, and himself most of all.

But to Scamp's surprise, this humanizing did not bring Mather within reach. Instead, it separated the two brothers farther apart than they had ever been.

The two walked for hours without exchanging a single word. Whenever the silence became too awkward, Scamp considered things to say just to break the stillness. Every time he felt the sting of his cut back and relived Mather standing by, watching as he was whipped, he bit his tongue.

The silence became a kind of law. It was wrong to speak. When they did, it was by necessity using short, small words such as "yes" and "no," and they never looked at each other as they spoke. It didn't take Scamp long to realize that even if he wished to bridge the widened gap between them, he couldn't. He didn't know how.

Eventually this distance between the two became

physical. Scamp, carrying Pug much of the time, walked ahead with Dannika by his side. Mather walked well behind, almost out of talking distance. He stared at the rusted hunk of metal Anden had given him as if it held answers.

As if Scamp couldn't forget the tension between him and his brother already, Dannika insisted on looking over her shoulder at Mather every minute or so. Eventually, even that wasn't enough.

"When are you two going to talk?" she finally said.

Scamp kicked a twig propped up in the grass. "When are you going to stop?"

"He feels awful about what happened," she said. "Just look at him, he looks sick. I've never seen Mather like this. And you aren't helping."

"Not helping? Really," Scamp said. "That seems fair. He didn't offer much help himself."

"You've got to forgive him some time," Dannika said. "He's your brother."

Scamp didn't answer. Instead, he grabbed the wyrmling's tail and tugged it gently. Pug was wrapped around Scamp's neck, his little round body balanced on one shoulder with his head resting on another. As they walked they'd developed this game: Scamp would tug Pug's tail and the dragon would hiss and squeal and start climbing around Scamp's body like a frenzied squirrel.

At Scamp's tug, Pug's head swung over the boy's

back, looking for what had grabbed him. Every time before, Scamp had been quick enough to withdraw his hand and hide it before the dragon caught him. This time, however, Dannika's chatter had him discouraged and distracted. His heart wasn't in it, so his hand was still within reach when the wyrmling spun around.

Pug promptly bit him.

"Ouch!" He jumped so violently the wyrmling dragon leaped from his shoulder. Flaring his tiny wings, Pug wobbled in the air until he landed. He then turned and hunched his back at Scamp. Lowering his head almost to the ground, Pug hissed.

Scamp stared at his hand. Pug's teeth were tiny, but he still saw pinpricks of blood on his palm. While they weren't deep, they still stung.

"He bit me!" Scamp exclaimed.

"Yeah, big surprise," Dannika said. "I don't see how you can touch that nasty little thing."

Scamp scowled at her. She'd been lecturing him since that morning on getting rid of the dragon. She said it was only a matter of time before the dragon set upon them in their sleep, and if she got eaten in the middle of a dream it would be all his fault. Scamp persistently laughed at her, saying she was far too big and fat to be eaten by anything less than a full-grown dragon. He then ran as fast as he could to avoid getting hit.

Now, looking at his bleeding palm, Scamp wondered if his defense of the wyrmling was justified.

He glanced over his shoulder. Mather was so far back, he looked like he'd shriveled from a towering, powerful man to a child. It would be no good asking his advice.

Scamp's entire life had been full of Mather's advice, offered unasked for. Scamp had hated that. Now he was surprised by how much he wished things were as they had been.

But they wouldn't be. From his perspective, they couldn't be.

Fixing his sternest stare on the hissing dragon, Scamp said, "Now don't you turn on me too. That's the last thing I need."

Grabbing Pug carefully so as to avoid a second chomp, Scamp lifted him in front of his face. Extending a finger, he batted the wyrmling's nose. "Bad dragon."

Pug blinked, stunned by the rebuke.

"Bad, bad dragon," Scamp repeated as he tapped the Pug's nose twice more.

Pug lowered his head and offered a hurt look. His hissing stopped and he started a low, sad purr. He even took his wings and wrapped them around his body and neck, almost hiding his head.

Then, without warning, he leaped off Scamp's hand and glided over to a surprised Dannika. She covered her face with her hands, trying to protect her eyes. Instead of an attack, however, Pug grabbed her torso and clung to her, wrapping his wings around her in a hug. He rested his head on her shoulder, refusing to look at Scamp.

She stared at the dragon for a moment before offering him an awkward pat. "There, there," she mumbled. The dragon twitched his tiny tail and purred, refusing to look at Scamp.

Scamp looked for another stick to kick. "Perfect."

CHAPTER 14

They walked all day, until the last glimmers of sunlight were so feeble Mather struggled to strike a fire in the darkness. When Scamp finally plopped to the ground, exhausted, he pulled off his boots and studied his feet, expecting them to be marched flat.

He'd never walked that far in a single day his entire life. They hadn't even stopped to eat. Whenever he or Dannika tried, Mather simply trudged on silently. He never said anything, didn't even look at them, but if they'd stopped he would have walked right on by and out of sight. So everyone had been forced to eat in pieces, nibbling corners of hard bread or chewing bits of leathery pork as they plodded on.

Eventually, Scamp gave up eating all together. After all, the ache in his gut wasn't comparable to the ache in his feet.

Now that they'd stopped, the emptiness in his middle threatened to eat him from the inside out. So when Dannika handed out the few scraps that were to be dinner—they'd been rationing supplies even shorter since parting with the peddler and his cart—Scamp nearly shoved her hand holding the food into his mouth.

As he gobbled, Dannika stared at him with a strange mix of fascination and horror. After tearing another bit of stony biscuit free with his teeth, he noticed her stare. "Fanxth," he mumbled.

She walked on, shaking her head. As she crossed the fire toward Mather, Scamp remembered the wyrmling.

Their spat from earlier in the day was neither forgiven nor forgotten. For the rest of the day Pug had kept away from him, occasionally beating his wings furiously in a vain attempt to fly. The rest of the time Dannika carried him. She looked uncomfortable the entire time, but luckily he never bit her.

Now, however, Pug was watching Scamp chew as if hypnotized. He stared at Scamp's wizened strip of pork hungrily.

Despite the gnawing void in his stomach, Scamp tore the strip in half and offered part to the tiny dragon as a peace offering. Pug hunched down, studying the wisp of meat. He bunched his small legs, coiled his neck close to his body, and began to stalk. Pug was awkward and indecisive, and looked comical as he hunted the jerky. His intense, focused look only made it funnier. Scamp was so delighted by the show he forgot how hungry he was or how his feet hurt.

He even forgot that he hated his brother.

"Hey, look at this," he whispered. "Danni, Mather, look!"

Dannika turned from her own strip of pork, which she was nibbling delicately. She looked just in time to see Pug hop one way, then the other, then leap forward and snatch the bit of pork from Scamp's hand. Pug rolled into a ball, clawing the pork with all four talons and gnawing on it as he tumbled in the grass.

Laughing, Scamp spread his hands like a hedge wizard acknowledging the crowd after a trick. Mather didn't look away from the fire. Dannika stared at Scamp and chewed.

"So?" she said.

"So!"

"How else would they learn to hunt?" she asked. "You don't think they start off raiding villages and eating knights, do you?"

"He's not going to eat villagers or knights," Scamp vowed. Pug had finally stopped tussling the pork—apparently it was sufficiently dead—so Scamp scratched his belly scales as he ate. "See. He'll eat pork like anyone else. And apples. I'll make sure he likes apples."

Dannika rolled her eyes. In mid roll, her eyes flared wide and white.

Scamp followed her gaze, asking, "What—"

His question became an astonished scream as he saw Pug hurtling toward his face with mouth open. He barely had time to cover his head with his arms before the dragon was on him.

Instead of feeling tiny teeth pierce his flesh, he felt Pug scramble up his chest to his shoulder. Pug then leaped atop Scamp's head, where he crouched low on all fours, looking like a scaled hat. Confused, but no longer feeling threatened, Scamp peeked through his arms enough to see Dannika staring at him and the dragon on his head.

With a tiny growl, Pug launched himself off Scamp's head onto a nearby mulberry trunk. He scurried up the tree. Scamp fell to his back trying to follow the wyrmling and barely caught a glimpse of him as he disappeared into the foliage.

"What was that?" Dannika asked.

"How should I know?" Scamp answered. "Maybe he likes to climb trees."

Standing up, Scamp searched the leaves for signs of the dragon. The greenery was too thick to make out anything inside, but patches of leaves were shaking so violently it was impossible to miss where Pug was. Scamp watched, confused, as the spot of shivering leaves went left and right, then started turning circles. All the while the clicking of claws and persistent hissing filtered down through the leaves.

After a few moments, the commotion stopped. The tree was silent and still.

Scamp stood on tiptoe, trying to see what had happened. Gradually, his curiosity turned to worry. The dragon couldn't be hurt, could he? Looking more intently didn't help, so Scamp decided to find out for himself.

Running over to the tree, he grabbed a branch and wrapped his legs around the trunk. Squeezing the trunk with his legs, he started climbing.

He was about halfway up the trunk when Pug shot out of the canopy and landed straight on the boy's upward-looking face. Scamp and the dragon both squealed as he toppled off the tree. He landed flat on his back in the dirt.

Pug landed on Scamp's chest. He sat there purring happily, a dead squirrel in his claws.

"Still hungry, I see," Scamp said.

Pug flapped his wings proudly and held the squirrel up, displaying his trophy.

"No, thanks, you go ahead." Scamp set Pug on the ground. He had to disentangle his tail from where it had wrapped around Scamp's wrist. Apparently, now that the baby had made him look silly, they were friends again.

"And bad dragons land on people's faces," Scamp said. "You almost killed me."

"Don't say that!" Mather shouted.

Scamp stared at his brother in shock. Mather

never yelled. He rarely ever raised his voice. Mather never lost control.

Until now.

"What's gotten into you, Mather?" Dannika demanded. "You go silent all day only to yell at Scamp for no good reason?"

Mather thrust himself to his feet violently and stalked away. His fists were clenched and he swung his arms as he walked, looking as if he meant to leave and never come back. Something in his eyes, a haunted look accented by the firelight, made him look like he was running away.

"Mather, wait," Scamp called. "I—"

Mather paused, his back still turned to them. "Don't ever joke about dying, especially not now. You never know when it's the truth."

With that he disappeared, dissolved into shadow and the whisper of footsteps in long grass.

Scamp looked at Dannika, who was staring into the gloom outside the fire guiltily. "I didn't mean to blame him," she said. "Well, I did, but not like that. I certainly didn't want him to leave." She curled her knees to her chin and wrapped her arms around her legs. "I just didn't mean it like that."

Scamp concentrated on the pain in his back. The cut was still long and raw, and burned like hot needles. But for the first time a matching heat of bitterness and anger failed to kindle in his gut.

"Maybe he didn't mean it like that either," Scamp whispered to himself.

The silver moon, Solinari, had made more than half its nightly journey across the sky when Mather snuck back to camp. He walked quietly, barely rustling the grass. He was so quiet, Dannika's steady breathing as she slept almost hid his footsteps. Scamp would never have heard Mather if he hadn't stayed awake all night, staring into the fire and waiting for his brother to return.

He was lying on his sleeping mat, rolled to his chin in his blanket. His back was turned toward Mather and he listened as his brother wordlessly unrolled his own sleeping gear and laid it out. Before Mather could get settled, Scamp rolled over and looked at him.

"Why aren't you ever on my side?" Scamp asked softly.

It wasn't an angry question. His anger and bitterness toward his brother had bled away as he watched Mather transform since the episode with the peddler. Mather's confidence and superiority had eroded, leaving someone Scamp barely knew. But that someone was his older brother, and Scamp had to know why Mather never acted like an older brother should.

Mather glanced at him without answering. Then looking away, he said, "I've always been on your side. You just expect that to mean more than it does."

Scamp shook his head. "All I expect is for you to try to help me, just every once in a while, when I really need it. Trying's all that matters, after all."

"No, it doesn't," Mather said. He met Scamp's gaze bleakly. "Trying doesn't matter a cracked copper in this world. People who say trying is all that counts are people who fail. People who try and fail get other people hurt."

Something in the way Mather spoke made Scamp realize he wasn't talking about others, discussing the foibles and faults of inferiors, the way Scamp so often interpreted what he said. The derision and disappointment in Mather's voice was oriented in one direction—inward.

"But . . . you never fail," Scamp said.

Mather shook his head. "You see, how could I ever be what you want if that's who you think I am?"

Mather flung out his bedroll and lay down. Perched on one shoulder, he stared into the fire. The fire's shifting shadows made his face look contorted in pain.

Scamp continued to watch his brother, at a loss for what to say.

Eventually Mather broke the silence. "Do you remember Grandfather, Scamp?"

The question surprised him. "Of course. I wasn't that young when he died. After the war, right?"

"Yes, after the war," Mather answered. "As if the war ever really ended for us."

Mather's voice was husky and soft and distracted. He almost seemed to be talking to himself.

"The conquered dragonarmies never really went away," Mather said. "At least, their soldiers never did. They became criminals preying on every peaceful person who crossed their path. It was worse than the war, in a way, because there were no officers or orders, no command at all. They did whatever they wanted because no one could stop them. Once, they burned our fields just because they could."

Scamp huddled deeper into his blanket, chilled by Mather's haunted voice and his own memories.

"It got so bad we started hiding things," Mather continued. "Food, what little goods we had left, everything someone might want to take. We started burying them out in the woods. I was with Grandpa out in the Esswood when a bunch of brigands found us. Grandpa said he was going to fight to buy me time so I could run away and warn our parents. I refused. He knew how to fight, but after his leg was wounded at Kalaman, he could barely move. He would have died.

"They took our corn, the only thing we hadn't buried, and told us to show them where the rest was hidden. I told them there was no more, but they didn't believe me."

Mather was no longer blinking. Instead he stared at the fire, in and past the blaze, to some horror only he could see.

"They brought out a rope and hung it around Grandpa's neck. Then they asked me again if there was anything else. They told me they wouldn't kill him if I showed them where the rest was. So I did. I started showing them every single thing we'd buried. Eventually Grandpa started yelling, cursing and telling me not to give them any more, that it was no good trying to appease them. I didn't listen. I told him I knew what I was doing."

Mather's silence dragged on so long Scamp thought he'd stop talking.

"Eventually there was nothing left. I told them they had it all, begged them to let him go. Instead they went to the nearest tree." His voice was shaking now, quavering. "They threw the rope over a high branch and . . . they killed him."

Mather's shoulders shook as he sobbed.

"Now you know why Mother and Father didn't tell you," said Mather. "Now you know why trying doesn't matter."

Scamp looked at his brother in horror.

Mather rolled over, turning his back to Scamp. "And now you know why I can't be who you want me to be."

Scamp felt all ragged and cold, as if something inside him had broken and a chill air was rushing through the hole.

"How old were you?" he asked.

Mather didn't move. "Seven."

Neither spoke another word that night. Whether Mather went to sleep or not, Scamp didn't know. He knew that he didn't sleep, not a wink. He didn't even dare close his eyes, too afraid of dreams of seven-year-old Mather sitting in the dirt crying as the brigands laughed.

CHAPTER 15

"Why do you think they call this place the Dire Wood?" Scamp asked. He looked around the forest of pine, maple, and aspen so thick some trunks brushed each other. The forest floor was carpeted in red and yellow shrubbery and vines, all climbing over one another. He imagined this was what the Nordmaarian jungles must be like.

"Because there are weasels the size of ponies here," Dannika answered. She used her willow staff to part the vegetation as she walked.

Scamp, with no such weapon, had to use his hands to push through the vines.

"Really?" he said. A branch Dannika had forced aside flipped back and nearly hit him in the teeth. "There are giant animals here?"

She nodded. "That's what people say."

"People say a lot of things," Mather said. "Doesn't make them true."

He'd been talking again since morning. Not exactly chattering, but at least he wasn't silent. He lumbered beside them, the chunk of dingy metal bouncing lightly against his chest. He wore it around his neck by its rusted chain, and carried Anden's other gift, his sword, by his side. The old, stodgy but dependable Mather apparently wasn't gone after all.

"So you think the giant animals . . . they're just stories?" Scamp asked.

Mather shrugged. He glanced at the tiny green dragon head poking out of the makeshift pack on Scamp's back. The dragon was purring contentedly, enjoying his ride.

"Who can say?" Mather said. "Father says dragons were just stories once."

Scamp looked around, trying to see through the dense undergrowth. It was no use. It was impossible to see much beyond their immediate surroundings. There could be weasels the size of whales out there and he'd never see them. Part of him was disappointed. Then he thought of meeting a badger big as a wagon and decided making it through the woods without seeing anything may not be so bad.

As Scamp waded through the foliage, he occupied himself with thoughts about Pug and Peda, and the tablet still hidden in Dannika's prayer rug. He even thought of Anden, who seemingly knew as much or more about this business they were wrapped up in than they did.

What was really going on? He couldn't figure it out. Who would kill Peda? It couldn't be that huge Bronze he'd seen in the Bristly Briar. Bronze dragons were good. And why kill for a simple dragon egg? There were a lot of dragons out there—whole armies of them clashed during the war. One wyrmling couldn't possibly be that special. And what was the writing on the stone tablet? A spell of some sort was all he could come up with. That thought always made him tingle, the way a powerful lightning storm can be felt on the skin. It also made him wish he were back home where there was no magic, no dragons— nothing worse than Jaiben and his crew.

Longing for Jaiben? Scamp shook his head, marveling at how quickly his perspective had changed.

He'd always dreamed of adventures. They sounded so grand—so, well, fun. But he hadn't listened to the stories well enough. He hadn't paid attention to the fact that people were hurt on adventures—that people died. Now he knew that all too well, but he still couldn't figure out what his adventure was all about.

Scamp looked at the wyrmling resting his tiny head on his shoulder. Pug had his eyes half closed, dozing. Scamp scratched Pug's chin and the dragon lifted his small head.

"How about it, Pug, do you know what all this is about?"

The wyrmling purred as Scamp scratched him.

Scamp chuckled. "No, not likely. After all, you probably don't even know that your parents are dead."

It was only when he said it that he realized it was true. That huge green dragon, too big to be believed, wasn't some mythical beast from a story. It wasn't just a monster. That dragon was a parent. And Scamp held its child—the child it died to protect.

Scamp knew what people would say to thoughts like that: Don't be silly. Evil dragons don't love their children. They don't protect them. They probably eat them whenever they can, the beasts. The only good dragon is a dead dragon, and once a dragon's dead, no one cares.

But as Scamp looked at the wyrmling and knew the orphan would never meet his mother, he cared. He cared because he knew other orphans from the war, and because he, too, was a child raised in violence. Most of all, he cared because when he looked at the wyrmling, all alone in this world, he saw Mather as a small child, all alone and crying near their grandfather's body.

"Whatever is going on," Scamp vowed to the tiny dragon, "it no longer involves you. You're not alone. And I promise, I'll keep you safe."

Suddenly, the dragon climbed up on his shoulder and extended his long neck. He was sniffing, Scamp realized. A moment later the dragon's wings beat furiously and he hunched up. Curling his neck in an aggressive pose, he stared into the forest and hissed.

Something was out there.

Scamp paused, futilely trying to detect anything but lush vegetation. He even sniffed the air, mimicking the dragon, but could make out nothing but the whiff of syrupy sap and rainwater. Everything was silent and still.

"Something the matter?" Dannika said.

"Where are the animals?" Scamp asked.

"Don't complain," Mather said. "The last thing we need is to spook a dire bear or something."

Scamp shook his head. The eerie silence was making him nervous. "No, I mean all animals. Listen. No birds, no squirrels—there's nothing out there."

Mather paused, looking around as well. "That is odd, now that you mention it."

Dannika closed her eyes and slowed her breathing. Scamp watched as a look of calm focus settled on her. "The animals are there." She opened her eyes, which were dark with worry. "They're just hiding."

Mather grabbed the axe from his back. Holding it tight in both hands, he peered about suspiciously.

"Hiding from what?" Scamp asked.

Pug started to growl. Scamp saw that he'd stopped hissing at the forest in general and had now focused on one spot totally choked with vegetation and hidden in shadow.

Though Scamp saw nothing, the dragon's tiny eyes had thinned to angry slits focused on that spot.

Then Scamp heard the hum. It wasn't a single type of sound, but many—whirrs, clicks, and buzzes all intermeshed. Oddly, it reminded him of the noise at Nallan Watson's beehives back home.

"Do you hear that?" Scamp asked.

Mather nodded. "Sounds like a hive. We shouldn't get too close."

Without warning, the hatchling wriggled free of Scamp's pack and fled into the foliage, disappearing in a shiver of leaves and lashing tail.

"Wait!" Scamp cried. He started to run after Pug, but Dannika's hand on his shoulder stopped him.

Her other hand reached out into the air, as if she could feel what lay hidden behind the greenery. Her eyes widened.

"Get back!"

"What?" Mather asked. "Why?"

"Just run!"

Before she could finish, something erupted from the brush. A great dog—a mastiff or dane nearly tall enough to reach Scamp's shoulder—burst from the bushes. It was black on black with a coat so glossy it shimmered in even the dim light of the forest. The only color on its entire body was two strange points of red light—its eyes.

The buzzing had grown so loud it was almost like a voice, but there was no other sound, no snarling or barking, so it took Scamp a moment to realize that the dog was attacking.

"Look out!" Mather shouted as the beast leaped for Dannika.

She sprinted behind a tree for cover and darted out the other side just long enough to swing her willow staff in a great arc toward the dog. The wooden blur impacted squarely on the side of its head, just below the ear.

Bits of the dog flaked off, filling the air like dust. The staff sank into the dog's head as if it were water.

"What is that thing?" she cried.

In answer Mather charged the beast's flank. He held the axe over his head, then chopped down using all his strength. The bladed wedge hit the dog's rump right where its spine would have ended—only the axe did not bite into flesh. Instead, the whole rear of the dog exploded into a swarm of frenzied flying insects. The swarm swelled outward in a furious cloud.

The front quarters of the dog stumbled, having lost its rear legs. The creature snarled, baring crickets and black wasps instead of teeth.

"It's made of bugs!" Scamp exclaimed.

Mather staggered back as the cloud of insects swirled, turned in on itself, and reformed the hindquarters of the dog. Once again whole, the swarm dog turned on its prey. Not knowing what else to do, Mather ran. The creature sprinted after him.

Scamp raced through the forest, following the creature and his brother. As he ran he scrambled to find his knife and darts in his pack. But what could they do against something like this?

After pushing through a copse of pine, Mather whirled, swinging the axe again. This time he used the flat of the blade. On impact a huge gout of insects spurted from the creature's shoulder. They looked like drops of water knocked off a soaked branch.

The beast convulsed, shaking back and forth as if hurt. However, it also snapped its false jaws shut on the head of the axe. Instantly, the axe became covered in insects. Mather barely managed to drop the weapon before it was totally encased by the swarm.

The creature kept coming.

"Hey, over here!" Scamp called, trying to draw it away from his brother. When the creature turned, he swung his pack straight into the creature's face. The pack began to quiver with all the insects colliding against it, and several items spilled out of the sack.

Spotting his wrapped up darts and knife, Scamp snatched them and ran.

The swarm dog shook off the pack and readied to

chase him. Dannika darted in from the side and swiped its flank with her staff. Again, insects scattered, but not enough to threaten the bulk of the creature. The beast turned its vivid red eyes on her.

"How do we kill this thing?" she cried.

Scamp had no answer. Instead, he fumbled the wrapping off his weapons, and cupping a dart in his palm, threw it. It hit the creature and made a small puff, as if the dart had hit sand. The creature didn't even look at him.

"Scamp, help!" Dannika was twirling her staff in the air, trying to keep the creature at bay.

Running alongside the swarm dog, Scamp threw another dart, then another, and another. Every throw caused another puff of insects. Finally, the creature focused on him. Dannika took the opportunity to dash away.

That left Scamp alone with the beast.

He ran, not caring where, just knowing he had to get away. Soon he spotted a tree with a lot of low branches. Maybe this thing couldn't climb? He sprinted for the tree.

Unfortunately he hadn't spotted the forest pool until he was in it. His feet hit the water in dead sprint, tripping him. The next thing he knew he was face down in water. Breaking the surface, he wiped his eyes clear of the stale liquid.

The swarm dog was directly in front of him, so close

he could see the millions of individual insects that composed its body crawling over each other. Its eyes burned red, points of fey light, not substance.

There was no way he could escape. It was too close, he realized, as the beast opened its jaws wide—snakelike—and lunged for him.

CHAPTER 16

The sight of the swarm dog froze Scamp, hypnotizing him with its horrid, writhing flesh of insects. He was going to die, he realized, and he was going to watch it happen. That didn't seem right, to just sit and watch the end come, but he couldn't help it.

Then he saw Mather hurtle from the brush to stand between him and the swarm dog. Mather held Anden's sword before him with the blade flat, as if it could shield them. It looked a ridiculous gesture when compared to the mass of swirling pests—until the beast's maw closed on the blade.

The chunk of dingy metal around Mather's neck flared in brilliant, silver light. A roar sounded, almost like the trumpeting of a dragon, but the cry was too grand and melodic for that. Scamp was awed to discover that the roar came not from the beast, but from his brother.

Suddenly, Mather began to glow. It was a pale white light, barely visible, but it surrounded him in a clear nimbus.

The swarm dog's buzz was deafening now, and it charged, ready to smother them. The creature's false nose touched the light and fractured, as if it had hit a wall. The huddled insects dissolved into a cloud, leaving the beast with only half a head. It reared, humming in agony.

"What are you doing?" Dannika called, peering from behind a tree.

"Like I know!" Mather answered. He was holding the metal emblem, which was glowing as if it were white hot. Scamp was so dazzled he barely noticed that when the swarm dog retreated from the forest pool, it was hobbling.

He looked into the water and saw the surface was thick with drowned insects—and he knew how to kill the creature.

While Mather continued to stand over him, glowing, Scamp tore into his brother's pack, yanked his blanket free, and dunked it in the water.

"What are you doing?" Mather demanded.

"Can you stop glowing?" he asked.

"Stop? It's the only reason we aren't dead!"

"I can kill the bug thing. But you have to stop when I tell you." Scamp ran to the nearest tree. Wrapping the sopping blanket around him, he started to climb.

"Scamp, what—"

"You have to trust me, Mather, or it won't work,"

Scamp said. "I'm trusting you. When I say 'now,' you have to stop the glow!"

Scamp continued to climb. It was hard with his hands slick with water and his body weighed down by the soaked blanket. Plus, there was still the swarm dog nearby. A glance over his shoulder showed it was standing still, its surface bulging and pulsing as it reformed its face. In a moment it was whole once more, if a little smaller for the insects that it had lost. Scamp concentrated on climbing.

Eventually he reached a high branch that extended over the pool. Wrapping his legs around the branch, he scooted out, shouting, "Danni, get ready to grab the other side!"

"The other side of what?" she asked.

Scamp looked down and saw the creature stalking Mather. Noting the dangerous glow, it started to look about for another victim. Its gaze had nearly spied Dannika, hidden behind her tree, when Pug dashed out of the brush and vented green vapor in what passed for the creature's face. At the chlorine's touch, the dog shape lost definition as insects dizzily fell out of place. In moments, however, they congealed once more and the wyrmling, having proved his valor, showed wisdom as well by hiding once more in the brush. The swarm dog returned its attention to Dannika behind her tree. There was no more time.

"Mather! Now!" Scamp shouted.

He watched his brother shut his eyes as he held

the chunk of metal in his hand, whispering to himself. Whatever he said, the glow disappeared. Seeing this, the swarm beast's buzz grew to an eager shriek. The creature leaped for him.

Praying Dannika would do her part, Scamp jumped off the branch. As he fell he threw the sopping blanket open. The water added weight to the blanket, but not enough to keep it flat. The far end started to rise. It wasn't going to work!

Then Dannika rolled from behind her tree and leaped out, snatching the other side of the blanket. The swarm beast hurtled directly between them beneath the dripping blanket, determined to immerse Mather in its biting, crawling flesh.

When he hit the ground Scamp tugged the blanket down, covering the front half of the swarm dog. Then he dived onto the blanket, driving himself and the creature into the pool.

It was terrible to feel the creature squirming beneath him, all those bugs crawling and beating their wings in a trapped frenzy. But as soon as he hit the water that all ended. The front half of the creature melted away, dissolved by the water. The pool was instantly dark with the drowned bodies of insects.

They had cut the swarm dog cleanly in half. The hindquarters staggered, wobbling and off balance. The middle of the creature, where the wet blanket had torn through, was ragged, with tendrils of bugs searching for something to grab on to. When they didn't find it the angry buzz grew into a shrill, panicked shriek. The remainder of the creature exploded.

The dog form disappeared into a thick cloud that dissipated within moments. Eventually, the insects scattered in all directions. When they were all gone, two fiery pinpoints of light remained, hovering in the empty air. The red pinpricks flared and pulsed with fury, but soon they, too, went out like extinguished candle flames.

From the pool, Scamp exchanged stunned looks with Dannika. She was so astonished she didn't react when Pug hopped off a nearby tree and onto her shoulder, beating his wings proudly. Then Scamp looked at his brother. Mather stood just as he had when he first protected Scamp, with sword extended across his body. He didn't look at all silly now.

"Not that I'm complaining by any means, but would you mind explaining what it was you just did?" Scamp asked his brother.

Mather shook his head. He almost looked embarrassed. "I have no idea."

CHAPTER 17

Seven days of travel by cart and by foot, a beating by a stinky peddler, a hatched dragon egg, and escape from one giant insect beast had brought Scamp not to another land, but what seemed like another world. He stood on the white swell of the beach with Pug by his side, marveling at his first glimpse of the sea. It was all worth it.

"It goes on forever," he said, watching the waves roll past the horizon.

Dannika grinned. "Only if forever can be crossed in three days. After that your prow would be tilling the New Coast."

Mather looked up and down the beach, trying not to appear impressed. Some people described that look as sophisticated, which Scamp took to mean disinterested in just about everything.

"So, we're here," Mather said. "Now what?"

"Now we find the home of newborn magic floating

on the sea," Dannika said. "Anden said if we followed the coast we couldn't miss it."

"Good," Scamp declared, "because if I could miss it I would, because I have no idea what it is."

As Dannika examined the length of coastline from north to south, she could not hide her concern. "We're almost out of food, so we can't wander around forever. Do you think we can trust Anden?"

"That question's a bit late," Scamp groused.

"We can trust him," Mather unexpectedly said. Both Scamp and Dannika looked at him, and he was clearly embarrassed by his confidence. His hand rested on the rusted metal emblem on his chest. "I don't know why, but I think we should. Maybe he earned it with this."

Scamp recalled the white light, the triumphant roar, and the swarm beast shrinking back from a glowing Mather. He didn't argue. "So, which way?"

"How about north?" Dannika suggested. "It looks like there's a jut of coast not too far. Maybe it's an isthmus."

"Is that the place where pirates hide all their treasure and grog under a big X made of palm trees?" Scamp asked.

She looked at him as if he'd just sprouted an ear in the middle of his forehead. "Yes, Scamp, that's exactly what it is. An isthmus is the place pirates hide their grog." She shook her head. "Come on."

Her mockery made Scamp realize that probably wasn't what an isthmus was. "I'd like to taste grog," he said defensively. "Treasure wouldn't be too bad either."

"There's no treasure and no grog, and I'm very glad of it," Mather said. "You're strange enough sober. I can only imagine what you'd do liquored up."

"Whatever it is," Dannika groused, "it would probably involve taking all his clothes off first."

"That was by necessity," Scamp said with dignity.

"All three times?"

Scamp grinned, remembering. "Yup, all three times."

They reached the jut of beach that stabbed like a thumb into the turbulent bay. Water stretched out on both sides of them, more water than Scamp had ever imagined. Luckily, it was not hard to find what they were looking for in the expanse.

In a shallow cove of rock lay an island. It was only a short distance from shore, and its green, smooth swell looked like a giant turtle shell. In the center of the island was a white marble building topped by a great dome, which on the backdrop of the sea looked like a giant pearl.

At the very tip of the rocky jut on which they stood was a small rowboat attached to a pulley system that crossed the strait between the shore and the island.

"Come on," Scamp encouraged, leading the way down to the dinghy.

"How do we know this is the place?" Mather asked.

"Why don't we try asking?" Scamp replied.

When he reached the boat he hopped in, lifting Pug in after. Then, thinking better of it, he tucked Pug into his pack. He wasn't sure, but he didn't think baby dragons could swim. If they could, why have wings?

He tightened the opening so Pug couldn't squeeze more than his head and neck out. The wyrmling wriggled and thrust against the opening, trying to escape. He looked at Scamp and bawled in complaint.

"Sorry," he offered. "I'll let you out when we're back on solid ground."

He quickly moved his face away from the pack to keep from taking a puff of noxious gas straight up the nose.

Mather and Dannika soon joined them in the skiff. It was only then Scamp realized he had no idea how to make the thing go. There was a board nailed to the front of the boat—the prow, Dannika called it. The end of the board fed to a rope that stretched all the way across the straight to the island and back, like twin laundry lines.

Across on the island, a stocky, pale lump of a fellow sat awkwardly on an overlarge chair that left his thick legs dangling. His chin rested on his chest, giving Scamp a fine view of his hairless head, which reflected light as well as the marble dome behind him.

"He's asleep on duty." Of course, it would be Mather who said it.

Standing in the front of the skiff and holding the rope for balance, Scamp called, "Hey. Ahoy ye island!"

"'Ahoy ye island'?" Dannika repeated. "'Ahoy'? What do you think you are, a minotaur?"

Scamp ignored her. It had sounded good to him. And seamanlike or not, it did the job. The fellow on the island shook his head and sat bolt upright. He promptly overbalanced on the chair and toppled backward on his shiny head.

It didn't seem to do him much harm, though. He was quickly on his feet once more, though it was hard to tell his standing from his sitting, he was so squat.

"What do you want?" His voice was deep and gruff, though an odd, high tremor sounded at "want."

"How do we cross?" Scamp called.

"Just sit yerselves down and hold on." The strange man rolled up his sleeves, showing arms as thick as Scamp's legs. "And don't buck about! This ain't no wagon ride!"

Scamp sat down and watched as the ferryman stepped onto a platform on the island, grabbed a winch, and started to churn it. Incredibly, as he did, the rope holding the boat crackled and sparked a bright blue. The boat lurched into motion so violently Scamp nearly fell back on his head.

He looked over the side of the skiff and watched the water rush by, amazed. They were moving as fast as a galloping horse. Startled by the motion, Pug shrieked and cowered back inside the pack.

The boat hissed through the water as it hurtled over the sea. Every time the prow hit a wave it reared up and crashed back down. Every drop gave Scamp the delightful feeling that his stomach had exited his body and was floating around somewhere above him. Their wake sluiced a giant V in the water behind.

"It's magicked!" Scamp exclaimed.

"No kidding," Mather said. He looked a little green in the cheek.

If Dannika felt sick as well, her lovely sable skin hid it. She had hunkered down low in the boat, though. As Scamp leaned over the side, she cried, "Get back in! What do you want to do, drown?"

No, but now that she mentioned it, an idea sparked in his mind. He knew as soon as he had this idea that it was one of those ideas nobody but him would like. He'd once had a notion like it, though, which involved a horse, a rope, and an old shield from the war in a snowy field. He'd known then that his parents would tan his hide for skidding about their field—and they had—but he hadn't been able to resist.

He couldn't resist now either.

Scamp peeled off his boots and stood up. Wind battered him, threatening to hurl him straight back down.

He held the rope above the boat for balance as he moved to the back of the skiff.

"What are you doing?" Mather demanded.

In answer, Scamp handed him the bag with the shivering wyrmling and, grabbing the rear of the boat, hopped out.

His bare feet began to skip over the top of the water. The soles of his feet stung from tearing through the waves, kicking up water in his wake. He barely noticed in his delight. It was like running on water.

"Try it!" he urged the pair in the boat.

"You really are insane," Dannika said.

Scamp grinned and zigzagged back and forth across the surface of the sea by weaving his feet. His grin vanished when he noticed those same feet were starting to sink deeper into the water. The boat was slowing down.

Scamp looked up to see they were nearly at the island. The round little man had churned the lever so hard his face was flushed pink. All his attention had been on the mechanism. As the skiff neared the small dock on the island, the man wiped his face and exhaled deeply, letting the crank stop.

"Uh oh," Scamp said.

The ferryman looked up just in time to watch Scamp plunge straight into the sea.

For a moment, all Scamp knew was water, dark with

shadow, and floating bits of weed and shell. The gritty water swirled and eddied, making tangled patterns even as it upturned Scamp, spinning him round and round.

He was just beginning to wonder which way was up—and how much air he had left to find out—when a thick hand grabbed his shirt. Someone hauled him out of the chaotic water as if he were a fish, only Scamp was a good deal more eager than he imagined a fish would be.

He broke the surface coughing. Wiping his eyes, he saw an almost perfectly round head without hair staring at him. The ferryman's face was fleshy and doughy pale, except for his cheeks, which were bright pink in anger, and his furious eyes, which were steely dark in contrast.

The ferryman was younger than Scamp had first thought. Even more interesting were his thick nose, small ears, and heavy brow, which combined to give his face a contour rather like stone. Scamp realized at once the ferryman was a dwarf.

After spitting out the water that had invaded his mouth, Scamp said the first thing that came to mind.

"Thanks," he spluttered. "So where's your beard?"

The dwarf's scowl turned to a full, teeth-baring grimace, and he dropped Scamp straight back into the sea.

CHAPTER 18

Scamp stood, wet and shivering, in the spacious foyer of the Thaen Thamateurgical Academy and College of Mystic History. He knew the place was called the Thaen Thamateurgical Academy and College of Mystic History because the bald dwarf made a point to pronounce the name very slowly and very loudly, as if he were talking to a particularly stupid dog.

The dwarf also told them that the master of the academy was named Galaban, that he was an archwizard of the White Robes, and that he didn't like bothersome guests, particularly dirty children. Scamp thought that characterization unfair—the dwarf looked no older than he was.

Maybe that's why he had no beard. Maybe young dwarves were hairless. If so, and given the importance they placed on their beards, it was no wonder the fellow was so grumpy.

And he was grumpy, no way around it. He didn't try

to hide it as he ordered them to follow him and not go anywhere he didn't lead, not touch anything, and stay silent so they didn't bother anyone but him. He never spoke directly to any of them. He talked at them, as if they were targets for his pointed words. He didn't even look at Scamp.

Still, enduring the dwarf's rudeness was well worth witnessing a place like this. The foyer was tall as five men and completely encased in paneled mahogany with fine scrollwork in steel. Bronze sconces in the shape of human hands dotted the walls, each holding a ball of flame. To Scamp's amazement, the fires burned without smoking and with no apparent source of fuel.

He couldn't wait to see what else this strange place held. Even more, he couldn't wait to find out what the whole adventure was all about.

"Just stay here," the dwarf ordered. "That means don't move."

"We know that," Mather said.

The dwarf stomped to the corner of the room and pulled a silken scarf that hung from the ceiling. A delicate tinkling sounded, like glass chimes in a gentle breeze. Then the dwarf opened a door on the right wall and disappeared inside. Scamp couldn't see what he was doing, but by his gruff mumbling he guessed the dwarf was looking for something.

Reaching over his shoulder, Scamp relaxed the knot

on his pack. Immediately, Pug's head shot out. He began to look around, from front to side to back, then up, then upside down over Scamp's shoulder. The baby dragon was wagging his head around so wildly Scamp was surprised he didn't get dizzy.

He noticed Mather watching critically.

"What?" Scamp asked. "He deserves to look too. Besides, he gets crabby if I keep him trussed up too long."

"You sure you want to walk around showing that thing off?" Mather asked.

"We're in a magic school," Scamp pointed out. "Dragons are probably like butterflies around here."

Mather continued to stare at him.

"What?" he demanded.

"You're dripping on the wizards' tile. They probably turn people into ferrets for less."

Scamp looked down at the puddle growing around his bare feet. Drat, he'd forgotten his boots back in the skiff.

When Mather refused to shift his gaze, Scamp snapped, "Well, what else am I supposed to do? I'm doing my best to drip up to the ceiling but it isn't working."

The dwarf emerged from the adjoining room with a thick blanket. "Here, dry your fool self— Reorx's beard!" he cried, spying the little dragon.

"Relax," Scamp said. "He's a good dragon." He scratched

Pug beneath the chin and the dragon closed his eyes and purred. "See?"

The dwarf edged closer, eying the wyrmling cautiously. "What color? He's so dark it's hard to see. Green?" His expression grew stern. "There ain't no good green dragons."

"Well there is now."

"Go on, get it out of here," the dwarf said.

"Now, just wait a moment," Mather complained.

"You just invited us in," Dannika added.

The dwarf shook his head. "No way I'm gonna let you hide a green dragon here. Who gets blamed when his parents come sniffing around for the eggnappers, huh? Hedar, that's who! Nope. Go on. Get."

Pug, sensing Hedar's hostility, arched his neck and hissed a warning. His tiny nostrils spurted wisps of yellowish gas.

Scamp protested. "But we came a long way for help. You can't just—"

"I said get!" the dwarf roared.

"What is going on here, Hedar?"

They all turned to see a young man with close-cropped black hair wearing a white robe. A belt with numerous pouches encircled his lean waist. A circlet with a small medallion depicting the academy rested on his forehead, and he held his head back and up, as if trying to keep the emblem as elevated as possible. The posture made him talk down at them.

The dwarf bobbed his head, refusing to meet the wizard's gaze. "Nothing, apprentice."

"Nothing?" The man's thin eyebrow arched in skepticism. He looked at Scamp, barefoot and dripping puddles.

Deciding he'd made a poor enough impression as it was, Scamp gently pressed Pug's head down into the pack and tied it up. The baby instantly began to hiss and struggle, thrashing at the cloth walls with his legs and tail. Scamp hid the pack behind him and tried to smile.

"Hedar, why is this boy wet?" the wizard asked crisply.

The dwarf's face paled even more. "Apprentice, it wasn't my fault. The boy—"

"You have been instructed not to tow the ferry at such outrageous speeds, have you not?" the wizard snapped. "You are permitted to remain in the academy by my master's charity alone, and you'd do well to remember that. Your meager skills do nothing to recommend you here. This is not Thorbardin, and you are no longer special."

The dwarf hung his head and bore it all. He looked so pitiful, Scamp wanted to speak up in the dwarf's defense. After all, it really was Scamp's fault he'd fallen out of the boat. But the wizard was so carried away with his speech, there was no opportunity to interrupt.

"If you wish to keep your place, outcast," the wizard continued, "then you will learn to obey orders as they are given. Do you understand that, at least?"

"Yes, apprentice," Hedar whispered. "Forgive me, apprentice."

"When you've earned it." The wizard turned to Mather, dismissing the miserable-looking dwarf, who shuffled from the room with his shoulders slumped. Hedar shut the door behind him, never lifting his head.

The White Robe eyed Scamp critically. "Here now, this won't do. Hold still."

The White Robe steepled his fingers in an intricate pattern and chanted, *"Pyrrhoa bal-canthian."* Then he lifted his hands and blew one quick puff of breath through the opening between his palms.

A warm, raging wind hit Scamp, nearly thrusting him back. So violent was the gust it reminded him of the air blasting at his back as he'd fled the burning briar, chased by the flames, ash, and sweltering wind.

A moment later it was over. Scamp felt himself from hip to the top of his hair, which was sticking out from his scalp like thistle. He was dry. Pug no longer struggled against the pack. Apparently, after the rush and roar, he was now content to hide.

The wizard examined the dry tile beneath Scamp's feet and nodded. "Now, how else may I help you? And please be quick."

Mather spoke for them. "We're here to see your master, this Galaban person."

The address clearly did not please the wizard. "Master Galaban is not to be seen by just anyone at the asking. What business brings you here?"

"We need him to help identify some writing," Dannika said. "We think it might be magic."

The wizard offered a contemptuous chuckle. "So you've stumbled upon a spell, then. Where did you find such a treasure, might I ask? In your grandfather's journal, in the attic trunk with the old infant clothes, maybe among your mother's forgotten recipes?" He shook his head. "I'm sorry, children, but my master cannot waste his time indulging imaginations. Nor can I. Find a traveling hedge wizard to divine meaning in your scribbles."

Over the years, Scamp had come to know that Dannika got angry more easily than some people. She hid it well, but there were ways to tell, particularly her mouth. Her lips were wide and full, but when she became angry they shrunk, becoming a little line that cut straight across her face. The thinner the line, the madder she was.

Right now, her lips were as thin as a knife blade.

She dropped her bedroll from her shoulder and let it unfold. Snatching the stone tablet, she dropped the bedroll onto the floor and marched up to hold the writing in front of the wizard's haughty, upward-tilted face.

The apprentice's eyes widened.

"Does that look like nonsense scribbles?" she demanded.

"Where did you find this?" the wizard asked in a cracking voice.

"It was given to me by a great man who died to protect it," Dannika said. "I promised him we'd bring it here and discover the truth, and not from some pompous apprentice who orders around beardless dwarves. Now, are you going to take us to your master or not?"

Scamp enjoyed the stunned look on the young wizard's face. Apparently, White Robes couldn't be evil, but they could still be jerks. Just to unbalance the arrogant young man that much more, Scamp removed his pack from behind his back and loosened the top. Pug's head shot out immediately and spat a gout of gas directly at the wizard, who nearly jumped out of his robes.

Mather walked to the wizard's side, close enough for the mage to realize just how much smaller he was than the youth. "Well?" Mather asked.

The wizard licked his lips, swallowed, and said, "Follow me."

CHAPTER 19

Scamp expected to be led to the master of the academy, and was very excited. It was only sensible, after all, to think that such a powerful wizard would be deep in a dungeon or in a high tower, in a room where the floor breathed, or ghosts swirled around the ceiling, or where the walls were lined with cages full of talking animals.

Instead, the apprentice led them to a trio of bedrooms. Each room contained a comfortable bed, a chest, and an end table near the head of the bed. No breathing floors, no ghosts, no talking animals in or out of cages. The beds didn't even dance. Apparently—and to Scamp's deep disappointment—they were just for sleeping.

The apprentice suggested the three rest while he brought the tablet to his master. Scamp didn't like that idea at all.

"We're going too," Scamp said.

"That's right," Dannika chimed in. "After all, how

do we know you'll take it to your master at all? You might pinch it."

The young wizard's face soured as if he'd just swallowed a mouthful of vinegar. "I give you my word."

"What words?" Mather demanded. "Because if they aren't 'come along with me,' they simply won't do."

The mage took a long, indrawn breath. "My master is in the midst of sensitive experimentation now. Disturbing him may be dangerous, particularly for the ignorant."

Dannika huffed. "Not so ignorant as to let you out of this room alone."

Exasperated, the White Robe said, "I swear by the magic and Solinari's light to deliver to my master what you have brought. Trust me."

Scamp didn't trust him.

Looking at Dannika, the mage changed his tack. "Rest and wash yourselves. There are tubs in the rooms."

Not surprisingly, the prospect of a good washing was too much for Dannika to pass by. When Scamp suggested that he was in no great need of a wash because of his dip in the ocean, Dannika looked him up and down and said he smelled even more like a hobgoblin than normal. She also threatened to wash him with her own hands if he would not wash himself.

And so Scamp found himself in a copper tub, up to his neck in water. As baths go, it wasn't that bad. The water was even hot. It started out cold, but when you pressed a tile inscribed with a strange rune, the water quickly steamed. Magic baths were infinitely better than normal, chilly baths.

As a rule, he did not like to wash, if only because there was no end of better things to do with his time, and the best of them made you dirty. He could not deny that sluicing that crust of salt off his skin was welcome, though.

He dried himself off and put his clothes back on. His shirt settled just in time for him to see Pug sprint into the bathroom and jump into the tub, where he burbled and frolicked in the water. Grinning, Scamp walked barefoot into the bedroom. Inside, he found the bald dwarf changing the sheet on his bed.

"Hello," Scamp said. "Is this where you stay too?"

Hedar glared at him so he didn't have to look up from the bed. "No. For penance I've been ordered to serve you three." He fluffed the blanket atop the bed. "See, I'm serving, so don't get me in no more trouble."

"Sorry about that," Scamp said. "I really shouldn't have gotten out of the boat. But walking on water is a thing you don't just pass up. It might happen every day in a place like this—you probably dance on water, all you wizards—but it isn't something a normal person ever thinks he'll get to do."

The dwarf's face contorted with pain.

"I'm sorry," Scamp offered. "Did I say something I shouldn't have?"

"Yes, but I'm sure you're used to it," Hedar groused.

"Do you mind if I ask you something?"

"Again, yes, but go ahead anyway."

"Thanks," Scamp said. The offer wasn't particularly inviting but he decided he'd take it because he really wanted to know. "Why did they think you were special where you came from?"

Hedar froze in the middle of smoothing the blanket.

"It's just, I wonder if it's because you're bald," Scamp explained. "Are you bald or do you just shave a lot? And are there other bald dwarves? Because I've never heard of one."

The dwarf abandoned the blanket with creases still in it. Flaring his shoulders, he muttered, "I am fatherless."

"Oh," Scamp said, not knowing what that meant but knowing from Hedar's expression it was hard for him to admit. "I'm sorry. Dannika's fatherless too. Her dad died in the war—"

"It don't mean without a father, human idiot," the dwarf bellowed. "I'm an outcast, banished from the mountain home forever. I have no people! This"—he massaged his hairless cheeks and pate—"is a sign of my disgrace."

"But why would they do that?" Scamp asked.

"Because, as you say, I am special. A dwarf who does magic. Lah di da and fairy's wings!" He flapped his hands and hopped about as he said this, looking mighty foolish. "What other reason could a dwarf have for coming to a cursed place like this?"

"You can do magic?" Scamp said. "But dwarves don't do magic."

"Not if they can help it, by Reorx's beard," Hedar groused. "And help it I can't. Whenever I'm around magic it just kind of sticks in here," he pounded his head.

Scamp eyed the miserable dwarf suspiciously. Maybe this was all a joke, a trick to get back at Scamp for getting him in trouble.

"I don't believe you can do magic," Scamp said.

"I wish I didn't believe it." Hopping onto the bed—it was so high Hedar's feet dangled—the dwarf rested his chin in his hands. If Scamp hadn't known that dwarves didn't pout, he'd swear the dwarf was pouting.

"You don't look like you can do magic," Scamp said, trying to bait the dwarf enough to make him magic something up. But Hedar wasn't cooperating. In fact, he wouldn't even answer.

Then Scamp had an idea. "You don't even look like you could make a mug of ale disappear."

"What!" Hedar roared.

"That's right," Scamp said, leaning closer to the

furious dwarf. "Not even a child's mug, where they cut the ale with apple cider. It'd put you straight on the back of your bald head."

Hedar hopped off the bed and bumped into Scamp, chest to belly. "I'll drink you under the table, human, you and all your ancestors back to Huma!"

"Fine," Scamp said. "Just magic us up some ale and we'll get to it."

Hedar harrumphed. "Shows what you know. Magic up ale."

"What?" Scamp asked.

"It takes a lot of power to make something out of nothing but magic," Hedar said. "And it's not exactly like I practice this stuff."

"Fine, fine," Scamp said. "Just do the most powerful magic you have." He had visions of balls of fire erupting around the room or gravity turning sideways.

The dwarf looked at him gravely. "The most powerful?"

"Your absolutely-never-to-be-used-unless-in-case-of-emergency most powerful spell," Scamp said. Then, thinking better of it, he said, "Wait!"

Running around the bed, he hunkered down on the other side, using the structure for protection. "All right, ready."

The dwarf took a deep breath. Then, reaching into a

small bag, he drew out a lump of candle. Setting the candle in his palm, he began to chant.

The words were thin and crawly feeling, like spiders, and the dwarf repeated the same phrase over and over. Each time he repeated the words a bit louder, and as the volume rose Scamp felt the hairs on the back of his neck stand higher. He crouched deeper behind the bed, just in case.

With one dexterous motion the dwarf flicked his wrist, turning the little bag inside out. At the same time he uttered a last word of power over the wick of the unlit candle.

Scamp prepared for something to blow up.

Instead, a chicken appeared on the bed.

It was not a giant chicken. It didn't have scales or fins or a snaky tail. It wasn't even bright blue or purple, or any other interesting color. It was a normal small chicken, with normal feathers of normal brown and white. It looked around the bedroom stupidly. When it saw Scamp staring at it in disappointment, it offered a standard cluck.

Scamp stood, feeling mighty silly hiding from a chicken. Hedar's pale face was slick with sweat, and he repeatedly wiped his brow to keep it from dripping into his eyes, as he had no eyebrows. He blinked frequently and looked a little lightheaded.

Making a chicken had left him dizzy.

"I see why dwarves don't do magic," Scamp said. "So they don't embarrass themselves."

"Do you know what that is?" the dwarf demanded, wheezing.

"A chicken," Scamp hazarded.

The dwarf rolled his eyes. "I know it's a chicken. Do you know where it came from? The forest Zhan, which surrounds the Hidden Vale."

Scamp knew the Hidden Vale was an outer realm, though he wasn't certain what that meant. He did know it was where Gilean, the God of Balance and Neutrality, was said to live, and that it was some place other than this world. Dannika had heard it from Peda, which gave Scamp reason to believe it.

Scamp watched the chicken strut around the bed with renewed interest. "So it's some kind of demon chicken, then?" he asked hopefully. "Does it breathe fire or eat cats or something?" Before he could check the chicken's beak for teeth, Hedar shook his head.

"It's just a chicken," the dwarf said.

"Oh." Scamp tried not to look disappointed. "A chicken from the Hidden Vale. Amazing. So . . . what else can you summon? Anything really big and nasty?"

The dwarf thought for a moment. "I suppose I might be able to manage a cow. Maybe."

A cow would have been better, Scamp thought, but not by much.

Suddenly there was a flurry of scales atop the bed. Pug, who had been content to soak in the bath with his head resting on the basin side, erupted from the water when he spotted the chicken. Hissing hungrily, he flapped his small, wet wings, flinging droplets everywhere as he chased the chicken around the bed.

The chase lasted for only a few seconds before Pug cornered the other-dimensional chicken. Before Scamp could grab him, Pug pounced, mouth wide open to receive the chicken's head.

Just before Pug reached the chicken, it disappeared. There was no smoke, no pop or flash of light. It was simply gone. The little dragon hurtled through empty space and right off the bed, squealing.

Scamp looked over the bedside just in time to see the dragon scamper back to the washroom and dive into the tub to hide his hurt feelings.

"Do humans often keep pet dragons?" Hedar asked.

"When we can find them," Scamp answered.

The dwarf shook his head. "I hope the master can answer the questions you brought him, human."

"Scamp," he corrected. "What's your name?"

The dwarf opened the door and paused. Finally, he said, "Hedar Stonesqueez—" He swallowed, and whatever he tasted must have been very bitter. "Hedar. Just Hedar."

"Well Hedar, I wish I could do what you can," Scamp said honestly. "Even if it is just summon chickens."

Hedar's face was grim and pained. "That is because you are not me. No dwarf would say such things, and no human will ever understand why." With that he left the room, shutting the door behind him.

Vigorous thumping at the bedroom door woke Scamp, at least partially. With his head still thick as porridge with dreams of dancing on water with tiny, beardless gnomes, he sat up.

"Hullo?" He tried to force open gummy eyes. "Did you bring your best galoshes?"

A thump later, and he found himself being shaken.

"Wake up!" a strange, shrill voice demanded. "Wake up, you're in danger!"

Between the shaking and the warning, he woke far quicker than ever he did at home.

Wiping his eyes, he found a young woman in white robes peering at him with eyes round as moons. They even had light from the red moon Lunitari in them. A wizard with red eyes. Maybe he was still dreaming?

"What's going on?" he mumbled.

"You and your friends must flee," the young wizard whispered, as if something hid in the shadowed room, listening. "Didn't you hear me? Go, now. They've found you!"

The icy fist that grabbed Scamp's stomach woke him completely. "Who? Who's after us?"

"Master Galaban is waiting to see you away," she said in a rush. "You can ask him. Now hurry!"

Scamp jumped out of bed and pulled on his boots. A small snuffling sound, like a pig happily rooting, drew his attention to the copper tub. The tepid bath was black in the dimness, but he could just make out a tiny green nose poking out of the water.

Plunging his arms deep into the bath, he pulled out the shrieking, wriggling wyrmling. The baby was clearly disoriented, flapping its wings and kicking to escape. Scamp's whispers quickly calmed Pug, however, and he was almost instantly asleep once more with his chin perched on Scamp's shoulder.

The woman barely even glanced at the baby dragon, she was so preoccupied. This, as much as anything she'd said, made Scamp realize it was time to get away from this place quickly. He didn't know who was chasing them, but whoever they were, they'd found Peda before. Now they were after the rest of them.

The White Robe apprentice led him in a jog through the winding, circular hallway that snaked around the academy. Her slippered feet swished in the dark, soft and subtle compared to Scamp's pounding boots. He wished he were quieter. Whatever was out there looking for them might hear him.

Mather and Dannika joined the jog through the academy, each led by their own white-robed guide. The trio exchanged nervous looks. Whatever was happening, it was because of them.

When they arrived at the academy's foyer, they paused to catch their breath. Waiting for them near the great double-door exit were two men.

The first was a lanky man robed in fine white. Unlike the apprentices, his robes were lush, multilayered garments with silver trim. The silver was cluttered with thin, spidery symbols of magical power. The tall wizard's face was smooth and narrow, almost gaunt, and ancient looking. His thin build made more sense when Scamp noticed the wizard's pointed ears.

The second man, beneath dirt from the road and a scraggily beard and hair, was Anden.

"I am Galaban," the elf archwizard said. He folded his arms in his sleeves and bowed in an antiquated greeting. "Forgive us for waking you, but you are in great danger here." Anden's expression, however, made clear it was no time for pleasantries.

"Anden, what . . . what's going on?" Mather stammered.

"Does it have to do with the tablet?" Dannika asked.

"Of course it's about the tablet," Anden said angrily. "Fools, why did you not give it to me when I told you to? Now they've tracked it here and it may be too late."

"And why were we supposed to trust you?" Dannika shot back. "You're the only one we knew was following us. You even said so."

"Peace, please, for we have little time," Galaban said. "I will explain what I can quickly. But do not expect to understand. There is far more going on here than any of us understand."

"Who's after us?" Scamp asked. His voice sounded weak and high and very afraid.

"Dragonslayers," Anden said. "Refugees from Tarsis, a city destroyed by the dragonarmies during the war. When they didn't find the tablet in your village, they debated destroying Tarban as they searched. Luckily they decided against it—for now."

Dannika gasped and Mather looked sick. Scamp thought of returning home and finding nothing but bodies and ashes, of once more having no home to go to. "They threatened Tarban?" he asked.

Galaban nodded. "And have followed you here. They wear armor of dragon hide, but their leaders I cannot see. A powerful abjuration protects them from my scrying. They seek you, however, believing you have this." He displayed the tablet. In the dim light of Lunitari it glistened as if wet with blood.

"Is it a spell?" Dannika asked.

"More," the elf said gravely. "The language you see is not the language of magic, it is even older. The second language ever upon Krynn, in fact, after the dragons' tongue—Kolshet. The language of an ancient ogre empire from more than 5,000 years ago."

Anden glanced at the archwizard knowingly, but said nothing.

"Ogres?" Scamp asked, aghast. Like always, when he said the word he thought of Jaiben. "Ogres don't do magic. They're too dumb."

Anden smiled, but there was something wistful and sad in the expression.

Galaban shook his head. "The savage brutes you see today are not the ogres of old. Back then, they were the chosen race of Takhisis, gifted by their patron goddess with beauty, majesty, and intelligence as well as great strength. Their empire was greater than any except perhaps cursed Istar, and lasted for millennia."

The archwizard grazed the tablet with his fingertips, as if he found the touch distasteful.

"There are no records from the time, but stories say that the ogres also commanded powerful magic—terrible, evil magic. This may be a remnant of such powers."

Dannika squeezed her eyes shut. "Peda was right. It is evil."

Scamp felt his stomach shrivel and drop. If the tablet was evil then what did that say about Pug? They'd been in the same chest. He looked at Pug sleeping peacefully on his shoulder. He didn't want the baby to be evil. He didn't want him to die.

Strangely, it was Anden who shook his head. "The writing itself is not evil." Seeing the others looking at him with interest, he fidgeted. "I cannot understand why this would be, given the nature of the ancient ogre race, but it is true."

"So if it isn't evil, then why is Peda dead?" Dannika demanded. "Why have all these terrible things happened, and why are we up in the middle of the night getting ready to run for our lives?"

"Because while the item itself is not evil, those who covet it are," Galaban said grimly. "I'm sorry I cannot tell you more, but powerful forces are invested in this relic of the ogres and they protect its secrets."

"But where do we run?" Mather demanded. "We're trapped. There's no going east unless we want to swim, and we'll hit the mountains if we head north."

"We can't leave," Dannika protested. "We promised that we would protect the tablet, discover what it means.

We still don't know. We promised Peda!"

Galaban laid a hand on her shoulder. "And you have fulfilled the promise, youngling of Majere. Safely have you brought it into my charge, and I will take up your vow to keep it safe from now on. Be comforted. You have not failed your friend." Turning to Mather, who he apparently took as the leader of the group, he said, "You are correct, young man. You must go south."

"But that means we head west again in only a day or so," Mather said, "right back where we came from. If they've spread out they may see us. Even if they don't, if they don't find us here they'll assume we're heading home."

The archwizard offered a gesture so slight and thin it could barely be called a smile. "Once they arrive here they will have other things to occupy their concerns. Now, those who have been tracking you have just reached the edge of the Dire Wood"—he looked at Anden, who nodded— "which gives you perhaps a day to escape. Go and make the best of the time."

No sooner did he say this than the night sky outside turned bright white. Immediately there was a sizzling hum, and Scamp felt the hair on his arms jump. Then came an explosion. The entire building shook, rumbling ominously as if groaning in pain. Marble dust wafted into the foyer in waves as they heard a distant wing of the building collapse.

Scamp ran to window, which was once more pitch black. He could make out the stars in the cloudless sky. Where had the bolt of lightning come from?

Then he knew.

Over the panicked chatter of the apprentices, Scamp asked, "Master Galaban, what if they have a dragon?"

The archwizard's face turned slack and gray, and his eyes held a leaden sheen. If he had looked old before, now he looked more dead than alive.

"Then you have no time to escape after all," Galaban said, "and we all may be dead."

CHAPTER 21

Fatima stretched her wings, catching the air and rising away from the great marble building. Her lightning breath had shattered the academy's only other doorway. There was now only one way out. Of this beautiful, ancient edifice, she had made a lethal trap.

"Drop off the Tarsians," the Black Robe called from her back. She was carrying fifteen men, between the vicious dragonslayers and the hated mage, and was only too eager to deposit her burden elsewhere.

Angling in the sky, she turned a lazy arc back toward the island and landed between the building and the ferry. Any retreat from the academy would come through there. The Tarsians dropped from her back like overripe fruit eager to be picked. She was no less eager for them to leave. As each of the bloodthirsty men dismounted, she felt a niggling itch dissipate, as if she'd just shaken loose a flea.

The Black Robe was last. He refused to even attempt

to dismount until Patima offered him her leg as a step, as if she were a parade horse.

As he dismounted she growled, "Remember what we've come for, wizard. The artifact. Killing is a last resort."

"As always," the wizard replied. When he looked at her she had that same strange sensation that something red burned deep behind the cold mist of his eyes, like a piece of coal embedded in his pupil. "But I will do what is necessary, whether it be bullying or blood. Will you do as much for your lost mate and children, Great One?"

"Do not mention them again!" More than ever, she wished to bite the terrible man in half and be done with all this wickedness.

The Black Robe simply smiled his typical bare grimace, as if even that much a gesture of goodwill was painful. "I simply remind you of your promise to me. I also avow my promise to you. After this night, a plague of vengeance will be loosed upon your chromatic cousins the likes they have never imagined. A revenge 5,000 years in the making! Justice for your loss."

It was what she wanted, all of Takhisis's dragon children to suffer—to die. They deserved it. The blood of her family demanded it. But when he promised this the words gave her no joy. More important, they gave her no peace. Her sorrow continued to ache as a giant empty hole straight through her center. Worse, this hole had turned into a ravenous maw eating away at her, and its teeth were bladed guilt for everything she had done.

But if vengeance couldn't make things right then nothing could. She could not believe that. She would not believe that.

"I will do my part," Patima said.

"Whatever it takes?" He stared her down, waiting for the vow.

"Whatever it takes."

"Good."

He slipped off her leg and fell to the ground so gracefully she doubted her eyes. It almost appeared that he had flown. She had no time to question what she'd seen, however, for he turned to her and gestured to the sky.

"Take wing and observe from above," he ordered. "This place burns of magic, so we must be wary. If bloodshed comes and I and our *allies* find ourselves in trouble, consider the problem yours to solve." He sneered. "Only as a last resort, of course."

Patima gave no response. She simply sprinted to the edge of the island, shaking the beach with each step, and leaped over the ocean into flight. As she winged her way higher, she had no question that the wizard's "last resort" would somehow come to be necessary.

People would die tonight, she realized, many who

perhaps didn't deserve to. She might even kill them herself.

She hated herself for what she was doing. But she hated her chromatic cousins more.

Hardening her heart—for what good was a heart now?—she prepared to dive once more at the domed building, death and revenge building inside her.

The gods had denied her vengeance. Now, she would take it herself.

CHAPTER 22

Another tremendous blast, like a star falling to shatter against the academy's dome, shook the building. The cracking of broken marble reverberated, bringing clouds of dust with it. The grit was so thick Scamp's eyes watered. He could barely see Mather and Dannika. Five other pale silhouettes huddled around him. They looked like ghosts, like they were already dead. Pug quivered in his arms.

He could just see the apprentice that had first met them at the door. He no longer looked superior or arrogant. He looked afraid. Scamp couldn't blame him. He was terrified.

"What do we do, Master?" the frightened apprentice asked. His voice cracked, making him sound much younger than Scamp had previously considered him.

"They will drive us from the building," Galaban said calmly. "Once outside, stay together and remember what I've taught you. Children, as soon as you see a clear path, run for safety."

He pulled something out of his robe's many hidden pockets—the tablet. He handed it to Scamp.

"Whatever happens, do not let them have it," Anden said gravely.

Scamp pinched the stone with two fingers, not wanting to touch it more than that. Pug had his head hidden inside Scamp's shirt. He could feel Pug, scaly and warm and trembling.

"But—" Scamp protested, but before he could finish, a *crack* sounded, as if the world were splitting in half. He looked up to see chunks of the marble roof, big as horses, plummeting on them.

Before he could do more than cry out, Galaban shouted, "Take hands!" Each apprentice grabbed one of the youths and touched the ancient elf. The elf shouted a few mystic words and the world flickered bright white, like a painting burned to nothing but bare canvas by the sun. To Scamp's dismay, he watched his own body become awash with light as well, until even he was gone.

Then they were outside. He felt grass beneath his feet, and above him stretched the starry heavens. It was difficult to make out even this much. In addition to disorientation from the teleportation, the darkness pulsed with the sounds of ringing metal and hostile shouts of furious men—armored men hunting for them in the darkness, he realized.

"Light!" He recognized the voice as Galaban's.

A feminine voice cried, "*Shirak entalitum*," and a yellow glow bright as daylight radiated out from the little group. In the light Scamp saw more than a dozen men clad in multi-colored scale armor surrounding them. The dragonslayers. Every Tarsian was armed with a vicious sword.

There was no sign of Anden, and Scamp could not recall seeing the warrior touch Galaban before the spell of teleportation. Remembering the fallen chunks of marble, far too large to avoid, Scamp's stomach fell. The veteran must be dead.

"Run, children," Galaban said. He calmly watched the dragonslayers circle closer.

"Run where?" Dannika demanded.

The elf stretched out his hands. "I will clear your way." A few whispered words later and a gale erupted from his outstretched hands, a roaring vortex of wind and ice. The blast scattered many of the attackers. A chill wall of air battered Scamp's face. When the torrent of ice died, one of the dragonslayers lay on the ground twitching, his many-hued armor rimed with frost.

"Run!" Mather shouted. Dannika was already on her way, so he pushed Scamp hard and sprinted behind. The trio ran through the gap in the line of dragonslayers made by Galaban's spell.

Scamp looked behind him, afraid for the brave wizards

aiding their escape. They had clustered together back-to-back, as Galaban had ordered, and were now surrounded by the Tarsians. But it was debatable who had trapped whom. Darts of light, fire, and bolts that glowed with dripping acid flew from the wizards, a constant flurry of deadly magic raining upon the attackers. Most of the dragonslayers spent more time dodging away than advancing, and those who did not move fast enough were hurled to the ground where they screamed in pain, or worse, lay utterly still.

When the Tarsians finally drew close enough to threaten the mages, Galaban swept his hands in a great circle and cried out words that made Scamp's skin shiver. A wall of fire roared up, driving back the attackers and protecting the small group of White Robes.

Beyond the edge of the magical light, Scamp paused. With no one around, he decided it was safe. Pug removed his head from Scamp's shirt, wanting to watch too.

Grabbing Mather, he pointed. "Look, they're winning!" Dannika stopped as well and looked back as the disorganized Tarsians flailed about as magic continued to rain down on them.

Then Scamp spotted a silhouette across the island, barely illuminated by the light. It was a lean, frail figure all in black, and two red spots shined like an animal's eyes from its hood. It extended a hand and the wall of fire around the White Robes simmered low, then extinguished.

"Find the children," the figure demanded. "I will deal with the wizards." Spreading his arms as if gathering the wind, he then thrust his hands forward. Out of the darkness a buzzing swarm of insects roared like a living, biting tornado. The din in the darkness reminded Scamp of the creature that had ambushed them in the woods. His sweat turned icy cold. The Black Robe had sent that creature after them!

Galaban chanted in turn. A hurricane's wind tore the swarm apart, scattering the disoriented insects. After the spell he staggered, just a bit, but too much to be hidden. His voice was thin and tired when he ordered his apprentices, "Go, protect them! Leave the Black Robe to me and do as I say!"

The apprentices obeyed, leaving him behind. Galaban and the distant Black Robe began to chant over each other.

Whatever came of the confrontation, Scamp had no time to watch. The dragonslayers had picked his small group out of the darkness, and he found himself surrounded by shouts of battle and flickering, multicolored armor. There was no place to run. Mather, with Anden's sword in hand, was fighting a giant of a man while Dannika swirled and darted about with her staff, keeping two at bay.

As if the press of dragonslayers was not confusing enough, bolts of magic, flame, and electricity flared as well when the apprentices joined the fray, throwing the island into utter chaos. Scamp even saw what looked like a dwarf made of dirt and stone rise out of the ground and begin to beat on the armored men with its stony fists.

In the tumult Scamp knew his job was not to be a hero. He had to keep the tablet safe, as he'd promised. So clamping it tightly in hand, and with the squirming wyrmling still in one arm, he ran farther from the light, determined to hide.

Before he could take a second step, a helmed face appeared from the gloom in front of him. Scamp dived just in time to avoid the blade that cut straight where his head had been.

As he hit the ground, he lost control of Pug. The wrymling leaped at the attacking Tarsian. Wrapping his wings and tiny tail around the man's leg, he began to scratch and bite, scraping the dragonscale armor with a piercing shriek.

The Tarsian staggered but appeared unhurt. Reversing his grip on the sword, he readied to skewer the baby dragon gnawing at his armored leg. Scamp stuffed the tablet into his belt, snatched his wrapped weapons, and tore the hand-kerchief open. Grabbing a dart, he sat up and hurled it just as the man raised his sword to strike. The dart pierced his neck, where it stuck out like a tiny tree limb.

Screaming, the dragonslayer staggered back, clutching at his neck. His sword lowered. Drawn by the blood, Pug scrambled up the armor and attacked the man's unguarded neck. Dropping his weapon all together, he fought to tear the wyrmling away.

Scamp looked around and saw no one else about to stick him. The night was thick with ghostly figures in white and shadows that glimmered with odd rainbow colors. In the background, Galaban battled the Black Robe. Pillars of fire, clouds of hissing acid, and giant spectral hands clashed, potent magics colliding only to destroy each other with such force that the entire island shook.

Then Scamp saw Mather and Dannika standing back-to-back, surrounded by four armed men.

"Come on, Pug," he ordered. When the wyrmling continued to struggle with the downed Tarsian, he said, "Come on! Heel or whatever!"

The wyrmling scooted after Scamp as the boy ran to rescue his brother and friend.

Sprinting in circles around the embattled twosome, he hurled darts at every spot of skin exposed by the armor. He stuck bare wrists, the backs of arms and knees, anywhere not protected by the dragon hide. One armored man, a tubby fellow who overflowed his armor like dough risen from a baking tray, he stuck straight in the bottom. The soldier started turning circles, howling and trying to see what bit him. Dannika's staff clunked him atop the head and he fell forward, unconscious, with Scamp's feathered dart standing straight out from his backside.

The flurry of darts drew the armored men's attention to Scamp, and Mather used the distraction to fell the giant he'd been fighting. One of the remaining two dragonslayers rushed Scamp with his sword raised overhead in both hands. Before he could bring the weapon down, Scamp slid straight between his legs and slashed a foot with his little knife. Simultaneously, Pug hit the Tarsian in the chest like a green stone hurled by a catapult. The armored man crashed to the ground. Three quick hits with Dannika's staff—stomach! hand! face!—and the soldier was unarmed and unconscious.

Scamp got to his feet in time to see Mather kick the last remaining dragonslayer in the stomach, doubling him over. Mather slammed the hilt of Anden's sword into the back of the man's head, sending him to the dirt. Mather looked around frantically for the next attack. None came.

Pug stood atop one of the fallen Tarsian's chests, fluttering his wings and preening himself in congratulations for his conquest.

Dannika rested her weight on her staff. Her face shimmered with sweat as she looked around. "Did we win?"

"Anden?" Mather asked, panting.

Scamp shook his head sadly. "What about Galaban?" he said, just now remembering the ancient elf.

He turned to see the white robed archwizard surrounded by whirling, deadly blades as thick as the stars above. A glowing wall enclosed the mage and every time a blade struck it, sparks lit the night. But the wall's light was erratic, pulsating, as if it were close to going out. Galaban was on his knees with the strain. The Black Robe was standing only a few feet from him now, guiding the blades with his hands and smirking triumphantly.

"We have to help him," Scamp said. Before he could run to help the elf, Mather caught him by the shoulder.

"Wait, look!" his brother said.

As if on cue, Galaban spread his arms wide and shouted mystic words. Two tendrils of smoke shot from his hands, winding out and around the Black Robe. This quickly spread to a thick mist, like a cloud nestled on the ground. Then the cloud caught fire.

It started as a single spark in the mist. This spark became two, which became four. Soon the air was full of fire, a small artificial sun surrounding the two wizards. Scamp and the others staggered back from the pulsating heat. He couldn't hear himself cry out over the roar of the inferno, and the air tasted so hot it scalded.

The cloud blazed for many moments, so long Scamp wondered if the spell had set the world on fire. Eventually, however, the flame dimmed. The lashing tongues of fire thinned and died, from four to two, and two to one, and one to none. Smoke almost as thick as the flame slowly covered the island, the only remainder from the cataclysmic spell.

When the smoke finally cleared enough for the red light of Lunitari to pierce it, Scamp saw a pale silhouette on its hands and knees, exhausted but still alive. Galaban. It took the boy a moment to pick out the Black Robe as a still, crumpled form lying on the ground.

Scamp twirled the knife in his hand and secured it in his belt. It was a grand gesture, he thought, and well earned. Looking at Dannika, he grinned. "I think we did win."

CHAPTER 23

The small group of victors—five White Robes, Mather, Dannika, and Scamp with Pug on his shoulder—huddled together near the lifeless body of the Black Robe. In the magical light he looked extremely pale, less like flesh than wax. His rich velvet robes were in tatters, with charred edges and whole patches burned away. The body continued to smoke. Mather, Dannika, and Scamp huddled close together, as if the sight of the corpse made them cold.

"Who do you think he was?" Mather asked.

"And why do these things?" Dannika demanded. "Chase us down, try to kill everyone. Peda. All for some stupid ogre spell."

Galaban examined the body and shook his head. He had an arm around his once-haughty apprentice—now filthy and worn—who helped him stand. The White Robes all had bloodstains on their garments. "I do not recognize this man," Galaban said. "He is no member of the Wizards' Conclave. Perhaps he was a renegade."

While the others continued to talk, Scamp heard something. A few somethings, in fact.

First, he heard a deep burbling that sounded like a boiling pot. That was Pug's stomach, he decided, because it sounded much like his own when he was hungry. Despite Pug's periodic whining, Scamp decided that breakfast could wait, considering all that had happened.

The second sound was so faint it was difficult to distinguish, and when he did, it made no sense. It came from the sky, a creaking and swishing that for some reason made him think of the whipping sails and rigging of a ship. To his knowledge no one had yet figured out a way to make ships fly, so he dismissed this sound.

The third sound, however, he could not dismiss. It was a scraping, a slow, erratic grind, like a malfunctioning millwheel, and he located its source as the collapsed academy behind him. Peering intently into the shadows of the ruined building, he saw movement.

"Look," he told the others, pointing to the spot.

In unison they turned to see a chunk of fractured marble fall out onto the grass, revealing an alcove inside. Out of the hole crawled a stocky, thick-limbed form, dragging something larger than itself behind.

"Hedar!" Scamp cried in relief. "You made it!"

The dwarf stood up and brushed off chest and arms, dislodging enough marble dust to fill a wagon. His bald head was smudged, with dirt or blood Scamp couldn't tell—it looked like a partially shaved potato, all lumpy and pale and blotchy.

Hedar offered a gruff harrumph. "Course I did."

"But you were buried alive," Mather said.

"Yeah, so? Weren't no big deal," the dwarf replied. He gestured to the body he'd dragged from the building by an arm. "Anyone know who this fellow is?"

Scamp caught a slight glimmer of golden hair ringing a square jaw. "It's Anden! Is he alive?"

"Aye," Hedar said. "He's got a crushed leg and he's bloodied up a bit, but he'll live. As cave-ins go this weren't so bad." He appraised the rubble that was once the academy.

"This isn't right," Dannika whispered.

"What?" Scamp demanded, turning on her. "Hedar and Anden are alive. We're all alive. It's great!"

"Not that—him," Dannika said. She was standing near the body of the Black Robe. The others had moved away at the arrival of the dwarf, nearer the academy, so she was all alone. She leaned over the body, studying it.

"What do you mean?" Galaban asked. He was clearly exhausted, but there was a thread of caution in his voice.

Dannika shook her head and looked closer at the body. She even extended her hand in the way Peda had taught her. She called it "seeing inside."

Whatever she saw inside the Black Robe made her leap up and grab her staff, ready to strike.

"He's pretending!" she shouted. "He's not dead!"

As she swung the staff, the Black Robe's hand shot up, catching the willow shaft. He barked a harsh, guttural word of magic and the willow withered and blackened, rotting at his touch. Snapping the staff in half, he rose to a knee and grabbed Dannika by the ankle.

Almost immediately the well-trained girl slammed a palm into the wizard's nose. His head rocked back, but then came forward again to leer at her. Smiling—it looked like a snarl— he spoke another mystic phrase.

Dannika never launched the kick she'd readied for the wizard's chin. Instead she began to shiver. The shiver became a quake. Her dark skin glistened as sweat began to pour out of her. Groaning, her eyes rolled back in her head and she collapsed to the ground, where she twitched and spasmed.

"Plague," Mather hissed in horror.

"Danni!" Scamp shouted.

He started to run toward her as the White Robes chanted. The Black Robe, rather than fight, raised his arms to the heavens and cried, "Now!"

It was only then, as the creaking in the dark sky grew louder, that Scamp realized the sound was real and was no ship's sail or rigging. It was powerful tendons and huge, batlike wings. The dragon.

A bolt of lightning ripped the sky in half. Galaban, apparently realizing what was happening, changed his chanting and created a glimmering blue shield of energy that covered him and his apprentices.

It wasn't enough. The bolt of lighting, a line of blinding light as thick as Scamp's arm, hit the shield and tore right through. The passage through the shield thinned the lightning, but that made little difference. A crackling aura veined with electricity momentarily surrounded the wizards. The next moment they were hurtling back, sideways, or straight up, trailing smoke through the air as they fell.

They hit the ground and did not move—even Galaban, who had a great dark mark on his chest.

The blast was so powerful that it knocked Mather from his feet. Only Scamp remained standing when the dragon swept down from the sky to land upon the beach, shaking the island.

The dragon landed between Scamp and the Black Robe, a towering barrier of bronze scales and ivory teeth and claws. Being this near the great creature was like standing in the middle of a lightning storm. He could feel the charge on his skin, and it made his hair stand up and dance.

Staring up at the horned head of the great Bronze, Scamp thought how beautiful the dragon was. He also thought he was dead.

"Give me the tablet, boy," the Black Robe demanded from safely behind the dragon.

"No," Scamp said. He was proud to have been able to manage it, what with an evil wizard and giant dragon standing right there.

"Give it to me," the Black Robe repeated, "and I will undo my spell on the girl. Refuse and watch her die."

Scamp watched Dannika trembling in the dirt, kicking and lashing her arms as her eyes rolled white. She was in pain. He knew it, and knew she might die, just as the wizard said. The knowledge made his heart hurt, a terrible pain in his chest as if a piece of him were missing. He also knew he'd made a promise, and to Dannika that meant more than anything else.

"No," he repeated.

The wizard smirked. "Brave boy. Dragon, eat this brave boy."

It was strange, but Scamp thought the dragon almost looked sad as it opened its mouth.

Scamp was trying to come to terms with the idea of being chomped to death by a dragon when he realized the head wasn't snaking forward to get him. Then he realized it had lightning breath. The dragon would fry him, just as it had poor Galaban and the other wizards.

Trying not to think of how much it would hurt, Scamp

focused on the knowledge that the end would come quickly. He was almost grateful to the dragon for that.

The Bronze's mouth was opened so wide that Scamp saw a blue glow begin to build down in the glistening tunnel of its gullet. The red walls of its throat began to crackle with energy, blue lines of power that grew larger and thicker as he watched.

He knew he had only a moment left and instinctively closed his eyes. Then he forced them back open. People always said, "If you have to die, die like a man." He didn't know what that meant, but he thought watching your end come might at least show a little courage.

With his eyes stubbornly open he saw Pug, who had fled at the crash of lightning, hurtle out of the darkness to stand in front of him. The baby stood with his legs spread wide and his wings flared, ready to fight. His tiny claws dug the earth for purchase. His head was coiled low like a snake's, eager to strike anyone or anything that threatened Scamp. He hissed insistence that he would not move, not even for a dragon a hundred times his size.

The huge Bronze dragon stared at the wyrmling as if Scamp had disappeared. The fey blue glow in its mouth dimmed and went out. Slowly it lowered her head and peered at the wyrmling as if it couldn't believe what it was seeing.

As the dragon's head—which was larger than

Scamp—drew near, the boy shuffled back and tripped. As he fell to the dirt, he covered his head with his arms in what he knew was probably the most futile gesture in the history of Krynn.

But the dragon's entire focus was on Pug, with whom it stood nose to nose. The baby was so small he could have crawled inside the Bronze's nostril. Despite this, as soon as the Bronze's head drew too near the baby green attacked, hissing as he bit and raked at the thick scales on the Bronze's head.

The Bronze blinked, not from pain or surprise, but to hold back tears. Scamp couldn't believe it, but the great beast was actually crying. Then an even greater impossibility happened—it spoke.

"My child . . ."

From his back, Scamp watched the dragon lift her head up, up, up, seemingly among the clouds. It stood straight and tall with pride as she turned to face the confused Black Robe.

"What are you doing?" the wizard demanded. "Kill them!"

"No," the dragon said. "There has been too much killing already. There will be no more."

"But the spell," the Black Robe hissed. "Your vengeance. And your vow!"

"Neither matter to me anymore," the dragon said. "As

for the spell, if it may be used by those foolish as myself and wicked as you, perhaps it is good that it disappear."

The wizard glared at the dragon in disgust. "Very well, pitiful Patima. Then I will take it myself." He glanced at the tiny Green that once more stood in front of Scamp protectively. "That lizard cannot protect you, boy."

The Bronze stepped between the wizard and Scamp once more, but this time she towered over the shocked Black Robe. Flaring her wings, she growled, "But I can."

The wizard was so furious he shook. It looked like something inside him was raging, wanting to burst out. Then, something did. His pale skin darkened and cracked, flaking open like a rotted peel. These flakes disappeared and from inside rose a horrid creature with blue skin and needle-sharp, fishlike teeth. The creature swelled, growing to nearly double the height of the false wizard. The creature looked like an ogre, but no ogre Scamp had ever heard of had blue skin and tiny black horns on its head.

More important, no ogre could do such magic.

"Deceiver!" the Bronze roared. Her head shot down and her jaws snapped shut. But the blue ogre had disappeared just before they closed.

The Bronze blinked and looked around. Then raising her head, Patima closed her eyes and seemed to listen. Whatever senses she was using to find the invisible creature did not work fast enough. Scamp found the ogre first when an invisible hand plucked the tablet from his belt.

"No!" he cried, trying to grab the tablet back. The ogre, once again visible, shoved him away. He kicked away the furious wyrmling just as easily. As Scamp fell he noticed the emblem on the ogre mage's chest—a tattered hood of bronze with two blood red eyes in the middle. The symbol of Morgion, God of Disease, whose servants were worse than any Black Robe, maybe worse than servants of Takhisis.

The huge Bronze turned just in time to see the ogre hold the tablet up in both hands in triumph. Then, grinning at the furious dragon, he uttered a word of magic and a flash of light consumed him. Another teleportation spell.

"Liar!" the dragon roared so loud Scamp covered his ears. "You have used me!" Bunching her tree-trunk legs, the Bronze leaped into the air and beat her wings furiously, flying north. Scamp was left behind, battered and disheartened. After everything they'd been through, he was the one who lost the tablet.

He had failed them all.

Soon after, he realized something even worse—Dannika was dying.

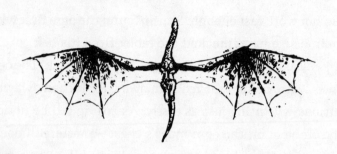

CHAPTER 24

As Patima flew, furious thoughts of the traitorous ogre mage and his manipulation swirled through her head. How could she have been so foolish? How had she not known?

Because her desire for vengeance had blinded her, that's how. She knew it with a deep, bitter shame. Everything that had happened was her fault. The ogre mage had used her anger and she had let him. She had been his puppet, and he had pulled strings to make her jump exactly as he wished.

No more. She had cut her strings and now the puppet would make things right.

From high above the coastline, she watched the contours of the shore. There! She spotted the dark blotch of a cave under the sea. Tucking her wings against her sides, she hurtled down into the water and toward her lair.

Ever since the ogre had first come to her lair in disguise, she had allowed it to be used as a base of operations as they searched for the tablet. Now that the ogre mage had revealed himself, she doubted he would be foolish enough to return here, but it was worth checking.

Using her tail to propel her through the water, Patima weaved up and down through the twisting cave. Her motion was almost fishlike. Bronze dragons were built to swim as well as they flew. After a few minutes through the twisting, mazelike caverns, she broke the surface of the water. Grabbing two juts of stone, she heaved herself from the sea, raining droplets onto the sandy floor of her lair.

Magical balls of fire sat in niches in the wall, illuminating the network of caverns. The flames created no smoke to clog her nostrils, however, and she breathed in deeply the scents of her lair. Immediately she smelled the putrid stink of ogre. The mage's magical guise must have masked his scent before, but now that he had abandoned the ruse, he reeked like rotting garbage and fish oil. The arrogant creature had invaded her home and wasn't even trying to hide.

Foolish.

Following the stench of the ogre, she wound her way through stalagmites, crystalline formations, and piles of treasure until she found him. The ogre mage sat comfortably upon her largest pile of treasure, reclining on a priceless pile of pearls. It was her favorite place in her lair on which to sleep.

All around the ogre mage, the cavern was littered with bodies of dragonslayers. The Tarsians' dragonhide armor had proven no defense against the illnesses that had killed them, which was clear from the pustules and bleeding sores that showed on their blank, lifeless faces. The cultist of Morgion had betrayed them all, Patima thought grimly.

"Your disease will not touch me, creature," she hissed at the reclining ogre mage. "Your god's foul curses have no claim to dragonkind. You should have thought of this before you betrayed me."

"Trust me, Great One," the ogre said mockingly from atop the piled treasure, "I thought of everything."

"Except for how to escape me," she said. "You are a monster. You have done evils beyond imagination and I have done them with you, to my shame. There is but one killing left—yours. And for this death I shall feel no remorse."

"Come then, wyrm," the ogre mage said. As he spoke he opened his hands, showing the tablet in his palm. "Let me show you how weak you truly are."

Standing, the ogre mage held the tablet in both hands and began to read from the dark face. As he read, the entire stone turned black, so black it looked like a hole in the world. Patima could feel that void sucking at her, trying to draw her in to nothingness.

She gave it her lightning breath instead. Taking a deep breath, she felt the electricity inside her crackle and spark until she nearly burst before exhaling. The bolt shot from her maw, a writhing, many-tined thing that filled the entire cavern with light.

The bolt hit the ogre mage straight in the chest. Instead of flinging his corpse across the cavern, however, the energy stuck there. It squirmed, like blue worms being fried in a pan, and as she watched, it darkened. The vibrant blue light dimmed, turned dull and brown. The corrupted energy slowed, became sluggish and torpid, like tendrils of sludge.

A terrible stench of disease and death filled the cavern, so powerful it made Patima's vision go black. She barely saw when the tendrils of filth gathered around the tablet and erupted to cover her.

She squirmed, helpless and horrified, as the loathsome filaments wrapped around her like ropes. Then they slowly began to seep inside her, sliding through her scales as easily as water penetrates a sieve.

As the foulness entered her she felt sensations neither she nor any dragon had ever felt: weakness; sharp, piercing pain; dizziness and disorientation; and most of all, a terrible dread that came from knowing, truly knowing, that she would die.

Her legs, once strong enough to rend stone, could no longer hold her weight and she fell. She was too weak even to lift her head. For some reason she was twitching. She could feel her tail whipping about, beating itself raw on the stone, but couldn't stop it.

She was so weak she barely managed to wheeze, "What . . . done to me?"

The ogre mage flew over and landed on her helpless, shivering body. "I've shown you what disease is, dragon. I have humbled you, as I will the rest of your kind."

Patima wanted nothing more than to destroy the vile ogre, nothing more in the world. Instead, she lay spasming and trying not to die, and barely managing that.

The ogre mage watched her raptly, relishing her agony. "See the power of Morgion, beast. Takhisis is a fool. My lord offered her this, offered to unleash his divine disease upon dragons everywhere during the war. Those who agreed to be slaves to him and his servants would live. Those who refused would die horribly, as you will die, my absurd Patima."

He wiped a finger in the wetness beneath her eye. The pain was so great she was crying, but her eyes burned as well, which made her think that the wetness might be blood, that her eyes might have melted.

"Instead, the Dark Queen decided to kidnap your eggs." He spat. "See what has come of her plan? Her armies crushed, the war lost. Now I will show her what might have been. Armies of dragons, chromatic and metallic alike, not in her service, but slaves of Morgion."

Patima barely heard him and did not really understand the words. She could not think beyond the knowledge that she, a dragon, was sick. Her flesh was infected, poisoned. She was dying.

Dragons did not think of death as the lesser races did. They knew they might die in battle, but that was all. There was no fear of age or infirmity, and most of all sickness, for dragons had never known sickness since the beginning of the world.

Now Patima knew it, and in knowing it she knew that she would die and it terrified her.

"Please" she begged. "Please . . . don't want . . . die . . ."

"Yes, beg, creature," the ogre mage said gleefully. "I can make it better—the weakness, the fear, the pain. I can take it all away."

Death was so near that she could no longer see him. She heard only his words as a vile hum and felt the putrid puff of breath on her scales.

"Live a slave or die free, dragon," the ogre mage said. "Which do you chose?"

She whispered her answer through tears—tears for what she said, and for her own cowardice.

"Good," the ogre mage hissed. "Then let's get you back on the wing. I have a little test for you. A tiny thing, a game really. How hard can it be to kill three children?"

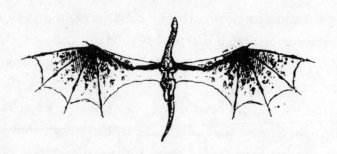

CHAPTER 25

Scamp used a scrap of shirt he'd dipped in the sea to wet Dannika's brow. Her skin was hot, even through the sodden linen, and she turned her face away as if his touch hurt. Occasionally she murmured soft sounds of pain, pleading for more than the caress of a wet rag. But that was all Scamp could offer. Pug occasionally licked her face.

With Mather and Hedar's help, they had taken Dannika and the still unconscious Anden to the east side of the island, away from the battleground and all the bodies. The east side of the island was a giant cliff with spires of rock out in the sea, like teeth jutting towards the sky.

They moved the unconscious girl as high up the cliff as possible to get her away from the carnage. Mather built a fire from wind-dried driftwood that he found on the beach below. Hedar watched Anden while Scamp did what little he could for Dannika—which meant sitting by her side on the sandy ground and wetting her head and watching her die.

Mather walked into the firelight with another armload of driftwood. Dropping it onto an already large pile, he said, "That should do for a day or so."

"She doesn't have a day," Scamp said, watching his best friend convulse.

Mather sighed and sat by the fire. He took a twig in his hand and broke it in half, then that half in half, until stubs were left. These he threw into the flames.

"Didn't you hear me?" Scamp demanded. "We need to do something!"

"Just what are we supposed to do?" Mather asked softly.

"I don't know!" Scamp was yelling now but couldn't stop. It was either that or cry. "Help her. I don't know how, but help her!"

Hedar cleared his throat, which sounded like two rocks scraping together. "Hey, this fellow's waking up."

He was right. Anden, who was lying flat on his back where the dwarf had dragged him, rolled to his side. Pushing himself upright on arms and legs, he shook his head. When he tried to stand, he cried out and fell, his injured leg refusing to support his weight.

"Take it easy," Hedar growled. "That leg'll probably heal if you don't go traipsing about on it."

Anden examined his bloody leg calmly. Then he looked around the island, using the light from the fire and the first blush of dawn. It was just enough to make out the collapsed academy in the center of the island.

"What happened?" Anden asked.

"We lost the tablet," Mather admitted, lowering his head.

"You lost it . . ." He said the words as if he could not believe them. "You don't know what we've done. My people, my god, I've failed you all—"

"I don't care!" Scamp yelled. Standing up, he pointed at Dannika and wiped his eyes. "I don't care about that stupid rock, or you, or dragons, or any adventure at all. Adventures are horrible things where people get hurt and people die. And these new gods don't care."

Mather and Hedar gaped at him. Anden simply stared grimly, his hand clasping the metal icon he continually hid beneath his chain armor. Scamp knew what that symbol signified now, that Anden was a cleric, and how little it meant.

"Paladine is letting Danni die and I hate him," Scamp said, breathless from his tirade and sorrow.

Anden's gaze shifted to the ill girl. His look softened, and moving gingerly, he crawled to her side and tenderly felt her cheek.

"She may die," he admitted softly, "but not because Paladine doesn't care."

Reverently, Anden pulled the hidden symbol out from beneath his armor. It turned out to be a small triangle made of a bright white metal, silver or platinum maybe. The triangle glowed more than star and firelight should have made possible.

Closing his eyes, Anden bowed his head over Dannika's spasming body. Scamp watched with tears untouched on his cheeks, daring to hope.

That hope died when Anden sighed sadly and shook his head. "The illness is not natural, it is magical. Morgion's slave has cursed her with a plague from the Abyss, and I do not have the power to cure it."

"Then do what you can," Scamp demanded. "Make her a little better, give her more time. With time maybe we can find someone who can cure her."

The cleric shook his head. "Illness does not work this way. It is not like an injury, where a partial healing is possible. An illness must be cured completely or the healing does not take. And this foul sickness is enchanted to infect anyone who attempts to heal it." He looked at Scamp sadly. "If I tried to save her and failed, as I surely would, I, too, would die."

Scamp wanted to demand that he do it anyway. That was what clerics did—they healed people, helped those who needed help, no matter the circumstances. What good were the gods if they couldn't save people who needed them?

But he couldn't ask Anden to die. Not because he wouldn't trade the man for Dannika— he'd die himself if it would save his friend—but because he knew she would never accept such a sacrifice herself.

"There is one slim chance that she might be saved," Anden added. With Scamp and Hedar watching on, he looked at Mather. "You can pray with me."

Mather stared at him, stunned. "Why me?"

"Because you have been chosen," Anden replied gently. He pointed to the rusted metal medallion hanging from Mather's neck. The furred lump could just be seen as a triangle with periodic glimpses of pure platinum shining from the thick rust.

Mather held the emblem in his hands, looking thoughtful and frightened.

"You can help," Scamp said. "Remember what you did with the bug beast? You're a cleric too. You can help. You can save her!"

"I'm not a cleric," Mather said. "I've never been to school or heard sermons. I don't even know anything about the gods!"

"Some people are born with the need to do right," Anden said. "They know others need them and how they can help. Those who find the courage to do so know Paladine better than any theologian or scholar."

"If your god can save her why doesn't he do it?" Mather demanded. "You're already here. Why not just use you to heal her?"

"I don't know," Anden admitted. "Sometimes the greater good, which is all the gods see, requires that we deal with great sorrow and sacrifice." He looked at Mather knowingly. "Then again, maybe there are two lives at stake here: one risking death, the other risking the knowledge of who he really is. That we are chosen is not enough, young man. We must choose Paladine as well."

Holding the rusted triangle in his hands, Mather stood. Walking slowly, as if reluctant but unable to stop, he went to Dannika, who still twitched and writhed in obvious pain.

"What if I fail?" he asked. "What if I'm not what you think?"

Anden smiled. "I once said you would never know the greatness of that gift." He gestured to the holy symbol. "You are not what I once thought."

Mather swallowed. "What if I can't do it?"

Anden's smile disappeared. "Then we will both die with the girl."

As Mather watched Dannika shiver and moan, Scamp took his brother's arm. "You have to," he begged. "Please, Mather, you have to help her!"

"I know," Mather said gently. Removing Scamp's hand, he offered a single, strong squeeze. "I always should have helped, or at least tried, no matter what. From now on—if there is a now on—I will."

He knelt by Dannika side. After a moment of hesitation he touched her with his bare hand, risking infection. He looked terrified as he did this but it did not stop him.

"What do I say?" Mather asked.

"Whatever your heart tells you," Anden said.

Together, the man and the youth bowed their heads and began to pray. Their words were whispered, far too low for Scamp to hear. So he sat near the fire with the wyrmling cuddled in his lap, and watched and prayed along with them.

Pug slept, making alternate purrs and hisses like a house cat, one moment content, the next riled. He occasionally flapped his tiny wings in his sleep.

Scamp found he'd closed his eyes and forced them open wide. Had he been asleep? He couldn't tell, but thought it was lighter outside than he remembered.

Feeling terrible guilt for falling asleep, he looked at Dannika. If she'd died while he slept he would never forgive himself.

Hours must have passed, yet Mather and Anden continued to pray over Dannika. But when he looked at her now there was a change. Her convulsions had stopped, and while her face still glimmered with sweat, it did not drip from her in runnels. She was still, silent, and pale in a way that he had never seen. Her midnight skin looked bleached the way things discarded in the sun turn gray.

Looking at her, Scamp knew she was dead, and even the glow of the rising sun would not warm him. Mather was even crying, weeping openly and unashamed as he rested his forehead against the lifeless girl's shoulder.

And he was smiling.

Suddenly, his head bobbed up, pushed by motion from Dannika. She'd taken a breath. As Scamp watched, not daring to believe, she took another and another. She was breathing calmly, steadily, in a way that made him know she would not stop for a long time to come.

"You saved her," Scamp said in awe.

Mather looked at his brother and his eyes shone with tears and something deeper. "Not us—but someone did."

Anden breathed a long, exhausted sigh and fell to his back. Despite his obvious fatigue, his face showed an otherworldly peace and satisfaction. Mather soon joined him, lying on the beach and reveling in the rising sun. The emblem on his chest glimmered radiantly in the dawn. The rust was gone, leaving a pure triangle of brightest platinum.

Seeing no one was watching, Scamp went to Dannika and kneeled by her side. He wiped her brow and straightened her braided hair, then tenderly kissed her cheek. Before rising, he whispered, "I knew you wouldn't die. I wouldn't know what to do if you had."

He stood up and wiped his eyes. After all, with everything well there was no need to cry. Only sissies cried when good things happened. Then he remembered the lost tablet in the hands of the ogre mage, and that everything most certainly was not well.

He couldn't bring himself to care. Dannika was better, and that was all that mattered.

Hedar the dwarf snorted awake with all the rumbling of a waking volcano. Standing up, he mashed his heavy jowls together and shook his head. Peering around blearily, he said, "So, she dead?"

"No," Scamp retorted.

Hedar spread his hands. "I'm glad, I'm glad. Didn't mean nothing. Sheesh, you humans don't do well with directness, do you?"

He put his thick hands on his hips and arched his back. He continued to stretch, complaining about having to sleep on sand, which was unnaturally soft and irregular, and so much less comfortable than a firm mattress on stone. Then he paused and shielded his eyes from the sun.

"What's that?" he growled.

Mather and Anden looked nearly as exhausted as Dannika, so Scamp was the only one who looked to the horizon. There, nearly even with the sun, something hung in the air, glimmering. It was flying above the sea, shining like a star lost in the daylight. Scamp could just make out giant wings beating, reflecting and refracting the morning light.

"It's the dragon," Scamp said.

Hedar gasped.

"Don't worry. It's on our side, remember?" Scamp said. "It's probably eaten up that nasty blue-faced freak and wants to tell us everything's all right. Come on." He tugged on Pug's tail, dragging him squealing from sleep. Scamp slapped his leg as he walked down the path away from the cliff toward the beach, motioning for Pug to follow. "Let's see if we can catch some fish for breakfast." The wyrmling trotted along behind him, apparently eager for a meal.

Hedar looked skeptical but eventually followed. So the two went on about their business, leaving Anden, Mather, and Dannika all sleeping soundly behind. None of them had glimpsed the black speck with a blue horned head that rode atop the distant gleam of dragon.

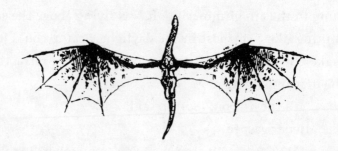

CHAPTER 26

Scamp dived and twisted in the surf, partially chasing fish and stony lobsters, but also just enjoying the water. Meanwhile, Hedar stood rooted on the beach, watching pale faced. Pug would dip his tail or a single foot into the water, but every time a wave surged toward him, he ran squealing.

Breaking free of the surface, Scamp wiped hair from his eyes. "Jump in," he invited.

"Not for all the silver of Shinare," Hedar swore.

"Why not?" Scamp asked.

"Dwarves don't swim well," Hedar explained. "We sink great, though."

"How do you know you can't swim if you've never tried?" Scamp challenged.

"Because dwarves don't swim and I'm a dwarf," Hedar explained sharply.

Scamp rolled his eyes. Keeping himself afloat by kicking his legs and paddling his arms, he studied the surrounding water. If he was going to catch anything to eat he'd better start being serious.

Suddenly, there was a deafening crash and a pulse rippled through the water. As soon as he felt it, something hit Scamp in the back of the head, sending him tumbling into the sea. For a moment he was in a swirling chaos of legs, bubbling water, and a green-scaled tail. Eventually he gathered himself enough to spot the sun shining above the surface of the water. Before swimming up, he searched out Pug squirming frantically in a futile attempt to swim. Grabbing the wyrmling by his tail, Scamp swam toward the sun.

He broke the surface of the water and gasped. Holding Pug free of the water in one arm, he struggled to see beyond the wyrmling's panicked thrashing. High up on the eastern end of the island he saw a lashing bronze tail disappear over the edge of the hill leading to the cliff. A smoking column stained the air.

"What happened?" Scamp cried.

Hedar, still on the beach, was staring at the smoking cliff in shock. "They're dead. They gotta be dead," he mumbled, seemingly too terrified to do anything else.

Scamp swam as fast as he could for the beach. When he reached it, he ran for the cliff. "Come on!"

Well before he reached the cliff he saw the truth. Mather and Anden, still pale and unsteady from their night of prayer, leaned side by side over Dannika's unconscious body. Circling around them, stalking, was the bronze dragon. She held her head held low with her mouth open, menacing. Her wings were flared, and she occasionally beat them, sending gusts of wind that nearly knocked the pair of clerics onto their backs. Most disconcerting of all, the blue-skinned ogre rode atop the dragon's back, calling orders.

Mather and Anden were kneeling within a blackened ring of earth. Inside the ring was a glowing white light that covered them like a bubble. As Scamp watched, the Bronze drew a deep breath and unleashed another gout of lightning. The ground shook.

When the light cleared, the ring around the clerics was darker, the smoke thicker in the air. The aura around the two still held firm, however. But Mather had fallen, and Anden had to help him up. Clearly, the pair was tiring.

"Crush them!" the ogre mage yelled.

Obeying, the dragon turned and brought her huge tail down on the tiny men as if it were a falling tree. When the tail hit the aura of light it ricocheted as if off solid steel. The tail pounded a long trough in the earth. Scamp felt the ground shiver beneath him. Crying out in pain, Mather fell and the light around the pair went out.

Anden had begun a spell of his own. Holding his holy symbol with one hand, he drew an intricate symbol in the air. Every line he drew flared with brilliant amber light, and when he placed the last line, the emblem burst into radiance. Flying like a projectile, the symbol collided with the dragon's chest. A webbed net of a thousand strands of fiery energy entwined the Bronze, who roared in pain. Staggering back, the dragon dived off the side of the cliff and took to the air, amber energy still crackling across her body.

The retreat was temporary, however. Scamp watched as the dragon wheeled in the air and aimed to fly over the pair of clerics. Patima's body swelled and another bolt of lightning shot from her mouth as she made her pass. Anden barely managed to summon a glimmering shield in time to deflect the bolt. Giving in to the strain, he fell as well.

The dragon hurtled over Scamp's head and started another large, lazy turn. Patima would come around again, and one last breath would end it all.

Scamp was so terrified he couldn't move. He could barely think. What could he possibly do to stop a dragon in flight? Then he saw Hedar at his side, gaping at the sky.

Scamp grabbed his arm. "Use your magic!"

"What?" the dwarf mumbled without looking.

"Your magic." Scamp shook him. "You've got to stop the dragon."

Hedar looked at him as if he were mad. "And how am

I to do that? Maybe some conjured bird songs will charm it down from the sky?"

The dragon had nearly finished her turn. She eyed the pair of clerics sadly, but still Scamp saw her draw in another great breath. The ogre mage's expression was a vile mix of eagerness and viciousness.

"Just get your cow ready," Scamp ordered.

"My cow?" Hedar blinked, looking as if he had no idea what was going on.

"Do it! Make a cow for me when and where I tell you."

Hoping fear hadn't completely paralyzed the dwarf, Scamp pointed to a spot in the air. It was just like throwing a dart, he told himself. Consider how the target was moving, how fast you could throw, all the angles. A cow couldn't be that different from a dart, could it?

He'd find out.

With a great beat of her wings, the Bronze picked up speed. She angled down into a slight dive straight toward Mather and Anden.

"Now!" Scamp cried. "Cow time, cow time!"

Though Hedar still looked confused, he started to chant. He focused on Scamp's pointing finger. Eventually he raised his own hand to point to the same spot. The chanting rose to a height and abruptly ended.

A cow popped into existence in midair. It was a fat-bodied milk cow, just what Scamp had wanted, despite the fact that it appeared upside down. It didn't stay that way. The animal immediately fell, tumbling end over end and mooing in protest the entire time.

The protests were drowned out by the deafening roar of the dragon when the cow hit the membrane of the Bronze's huge right wing. The wing crumpled like a spread blanket with a boulder on it. The dragon, ogre mage, and cow all plummeted to the ground, though the cow disappeared before it landed.

The dragon and ogre certainly did hit the ground, and with a thump that bounced Scamp straight off his feet.

"Reorx's beard!" Hedar gasped. "I killed a dragon with a cow!"

"Killed" was an exaggeration. The huge Bronze was alive—and furious. Patima kicked and lashed her tail, trying to untangle herself and get back to her feet. The tattered, broken wing that hung limply at her side made this more difficult.

The ogre mage had been thrown free during the fall. Scamp finally found him a good distance away at the end of a furrowed trail the creature had made tumbling over the earth. The ogre was on his hands and knees, shaking his head. Then a look of panic swept over his cruel face. He began to tear through the many pockets of his filthy robes. When that didn't work he felt every inch of his body over for what he had lost.

Scamp found the item before the ogre mage did. Lying alone and unnoticed in a patch of wizened grass, directly between the fallen dragon and ogre, was the tablet.

CHAPTER 27

The dragon continued to roar and thrash the ground. It was like being in an earthquake. Over this tumult Scamp barely heard Anden cry, "Get the tablet! Its spell controls the dragon!"

Scamp stared at the stone, wondering how such a tiny thing could master a dragon. Then he saw the ogre mage rise to his feet. No more time to think. He sprinted.

If he had allowed time to think, it may have occurred to him that the stone lay directly between the cultist and the flailing dragon, in a kind of alley beset by lashing wings and a tail thick as an oak trunk that kept pummeling the ground. Also, the ogre mage was on his feet now, and closer to the tablet than Scamp. If they should meet at the item, a huge magical ogre against the sopping boy, it wasn't hard to imagine what might happen, and all possibilities were bad. Finally, the stone and its bed of wizened grass were situated right on the cliff edge. If he somehow got the stone, what then? There was nowhere to go.

Thankfully for all involved that day, Scamp was prone to act before he thought. Before he could think better of it, he was sprinting into that alley of mashing, smashing dragon flesh.

The ogre mage saw Scamp running and finally noticed the tablet lying in the grass. Snarling, and with his eyes bulging as if to pop out and roll to the item first, the ogre mage leaped into the air. He never came down. Flying without wings, he hurtled toward the stone tablet.

Scamp ran as fast as he could, but the kicking hind legs and lashing tail of the dragon complicated his path. The Bronze was still half on the ground, trying to untangle herself from her broken wing. Patima's thrashings dug great furrows in the ground and tossed waves of sandy soil through the air. It was all Scamp could do to peer through the grit enough to see that thick mast of a tail clubbing the hillside, and if he didn't move fast enough, Scamp's head.

The boy ducked, dived, and rolled on the ground to escape the dragon's fit. He zigged and zagged as he ran toward the cliff, blinking to see through the haze of dirt and spitting out mouthfuls as he panted.

Finally, he passed the furious dragon. A terrible sight awaited him: the ogre mage was alight on the ground next to the stone. He sneered in triumph, baring thin, sharklike teeth, an expression that made him even fouler.

Scamp watched in despair as the creature bent down for the tablet. He could never reach it now. Unless . . .

In one smooth motion, the way he always played the game in Peda's yard, Scamp grabbed one of the tiny darts from his belt and threw. He didn't even stop running.

The dart buried itself in the ogre's forearm, just above the wrist. It pierced so deep it actually pinned the filthy velvet sleeve to the ogre's arm. The creature screamed and tottered back, staring at the fletching in shock, as if it had sprouted there.

The ogre mage recovered just in time to see Scamp duck in mid-sprint to snatch the tablet from the ground. Digging his heels into the earth so deeply he nearly fell, Scamp turned away from the furious ogre. He didn't know where he could go, but he started running for all he was worth.

"Get the spell, slave!" the ogre mage shouted. "Kill the boy, or else!"

The dragon, finally back on her feet, took two huge steps, blocking Scamp's way. Patima spread her healthy wing, cutting him off completely from the rest of the island. With the cliff at his back and the dragon towering over him everywhere else, he stood still. There was nowhere to go. The dragon coiled her neck to strike and Scamp felt his stomach migrate somewhere else, leaving a cold little nook where his belly had been.

His options were bad, but they were simple: the dragon or the cliff. He watched the dragon open her maw and saw all those bladed, ivory teeth, and this decided it.

Turning around, he sprinted for the cliff edge.

"Stop him!" the ogre cried.

The dragon's head shot forward fast as an arrow from a bow. Luckily, Scamp had moved first. He continued sprinting for the cliff and could not keep from screaming as he ran straight off the edge. The dragon's mouth clamped shut behind him, her teeth grinding like steel scouring steel.

Scamp had a moment to wonder, now that he was falling, where he might land. Then he saw one of the spires of stone stabbing up from the ocean. Stretching out, he caught a lip of boulder and swung onto the rocky overhang. His belly hit the stone, driving his breath away.

He looked around and saw dozens of stone spines stabbing up from the sea. Some were lower than the one he held, some higher; each had a tiny, flat top like a filed-down tip of a tooth.

The dragon bellowed from the cliff above. He heard heavy footsteps shaking the ground. Patima was coming for him.

He scrambled up the spire until he reached the top. Ignoring the roaring behind him, which grew louder rapidly, he balanced carefully on both feet and aimed for another pillar of rock. He leaped.

The ocean below him sparkled, as if eager for him to fall, and it seemed he would because no way could a jump last this long. Eventually, however, he landed on another stone spine. One foot slipped. He windmilled his arms, fighting for balance. It was probably as much luck as dexterity that saved him from a fall.

Glancing over his shoulder, he saw the dragon hurl herself off the cliff edge. The dragon hit the spire he had jumped from, which shattered, filling the air with chunks of stone bigger than Scamp. The sea roiled and frothed from the falling blocks. The dragon paid no attention to the stone ricocheting off her scaly hide. Patima grabbed two other pillars and wound her tail around a third to support her great weight. Her head snaked back and forth and around the columns of stone, searching for Scamp.

He fled wherever he could. He jumped from spire to spire, sometimes landing feet first on top, sometimes clinging to the side by his fingernails. The stone tablet in his hand only made things harder. The dragon, on the other hand, was so large she climbed from column to column, winding her way through the needlelike maze like a snake.

Scamp continued to hurl himself from rock to rock, though he knew it was hopeless. He was so tired that his chest felt as if he'd swallowed live coals. His hands were bruised and bleeding. It was only a matter of time before he would slip and fall to be dashed to death by the waves.

Or before that, to be caught by the dragon and eaten in one great bite.

Leaping to another stone spire, one of the largest, he inched his way around behind it. Putting the rock between him and the dragon would hide him, he hoped, and give him a moment to think.

He stared at the stone tablet clutched in his bleeding fingers. He could drop it, he realized. Give it to the sea. Looking down, he watched how the morning light fractured and dimmed in the water, dying as it tried and failed to reach the ocean depths. It looked deep. There was a chance the tablet would never be found on the sea floor. It might be safe. He was already dead, but knowing the spell was out of the ogre's reach would make dying worthwhile. He wanted his death to matter in some way, at least a little.

He readied to drop the tablet. Just as he was about to loosen his fingers and watch the stone drop, he heard a voice cry out, "No!"

Looking to the cliff he saw Anden standing at the edge. Cupping his hands at his mouth, the man shouted, "We have to reverse the spell to free the dragon. Throw the stone!" The cleric opened his arms, making himself a target.

The dragon's clamor was deafening: scales scraping against rock, claws tearing stone, roars like a thousand lions pent up in a single canyon. Scamp's head rang from the noise. He grew dizzy. He didn't need to peek around his stone shield to know that he'd been found out and the dragon was coming for him. He could hear her, the grate and grind of the giant body climbing nearer.

Drawing back his arm, he threw the tablet as hard as he could. Just as the stone left his fingers the rocky spire he clung to exploded. The dragon dived straight through the stone, shoulder first, fracturing it into a thousand pieces. Those thousand pieces fell with Scamp, and the dragon plummeted down right along with them.

Scamp watched the dragon open her maw to engulf him. He looked away. He had to know if the tablet was safe, if he'd succeeded.

The tablet was spinning through the air almost lazily. Eventually, after a lifetime of falling, it reached the cliff edge. Anden reached up to grab the stone. Another pair of hands, blue with thick black claws, met his.

The ogre mage and Anden looked at each other. Each held one side of the tablet. The ogre mage smirked and tried to pull away his prize. It should have been easy, a giant ogre against a normal man, like taking candy from a toddler. Anden's grip did not give and his arm did not shiver. Both stayed as strong as the stone they held.

The ogre mage looked at the cleric in surprise. This surprise turned to shock as Anden shimmered, like an image in a pool, and disappeared. In his place was a spectacular being: skin like sapphire laced with ivory and hair of spun sterling. It had delicate pointed ears, almost like elf ears, and thimble pools of molten silver for eyes. The being had an otherworldly beauty, beyond natural, like a perfect marble sculpture brought to life.

That was all the more startling when, side by side with the horrid ogre mage, Scamp realized these beings were kin. One was a twisted, spoiled reflection of the other. The elegant creature was an ogre too.

The ogre mage had only a moment to stare at its lost cousin. Then, from nowhere, a tornado of tiny green scales and flashing claws was on the ogre mage's face. He stumbled, trying to tear the wyrmling away. It was no good. Pug was moving so frantically he didn't look material, just a green blur in an ever-glowing cloud of chlorine gas.

Anden—or the being that had once been Anden—raised the tablet above his head and began to chant. The stone glowed so brightly it was as if he held a sliver of sun. Then Scamp's view was blocked by a mountain of bronze with furious, slitted eyes and teeth long as his forearm.

Relaxing, Scamp let his arms and legs hang loose as he fell. In the moment before the dragon struck, he reveled in the sensation of falling with the knowledge he would never land. It was like flying, he realized. Wasn't that what flying was, falling through the air with the knowledge you never had to come down?

He would die flying. It was enough to make him smile as the dragon's head shot forward.

He was nearly in the dragon's mouth when the beast's eyes, large as dinner plates, shimmered. A fetid brown stain that he hadn't noticed before, a churning sludge in the whites of her eyes, disappeared. The dragon blinked. When she opened her eyes once more they shone like molten metal and radiated joy.

Instead of the jaws engulfing him, a great claw gently snatched him from the air. The dragon cradled him to her chest as she snagged a nearby pillar of stone and stopped their fall. Scamp watched the ocean waves pulse beneath him, so near he could smell the salt. Reaching out with one hand he brushed the waves before the dragon climbed back up the cliff, carrying him protectively.

Before they crested the cliff, the dragon snaked her head near Scamp and whispered, "Thank you, child."

Then the dragon heaved her great bulk back atop the cliff. Setting Scamp down gently, the dragon raised her head proudly. Patima's molten eyes searched out the evil mage.

The ogre had finally freed himself of the furious wyrmling, which he held in his clawed hands. The ogre was squeezing the wyrmling's neck, choking him mercilessly. Pug writhed helplessly and cried for help.

"Hey," Scamp shouted, "that's my dragon!"

The mage looked up, stunned that he lived. That

moment was all Pug needed. Squirming loose, the baby vented a puff of yellow-green gas directly in the ogre's face. He gasped and dropped the wyrmling to claw at his burning eyes.

"Come here, Pug," Scamp called. The wyrmling saw him and, beating his wings happily, hopped into Scamp's arms. He stroked the dragon as the wyrmling rested his head on Scamp's shoulder.

As the giant Bronze bore down on the blinded cultist, Scamp turned his body to shield Pug from the scene to come. "Let's let a bigger dragon handle this."

Scamp and the ogre Anden, with Hedar and Mather farther down the cliff, stood and watched as the ogre finally cleared his eyes. He looked up to see the bronze dragon towering over him and for the first time, the look of cruel superiority on the ogre's face dissolved, revealing panic. At the last moment he tried to turn invisible. His hands and legs faded away, and the rest of his body began to dissolve as well, like a mirage coming undone.

The dragon struck faster than Scamp could see. One moment she glowered down on the ogre cultist, the next there was a streak of bronze and the clash of massive teeth. When the dragon lifted her head again, the follower of Morgion was gone. His scream, suddenly cut off as if by a blade, let Scamp know that this time he had not simply disappeared, and would never reappear again.

CHAPTER 28

From atop the flying Patima—Anden and Mather had healed her broken wing—Scamp looked down on a world that suddenly seemed much smaller than before. For some reason, after this adventure, he thought it would always be smaller, even when he set foot on ground again.

Until that time, he would enjoy the greatest adventure of his life.

As they flew, the ogre Anden told them the story of the tablet—a story, Scamp realized, that was now his story as well.

"Millennia ago in the Age of Starlight, the ogres reigned on Krynn," Anden said. His voice was gentle and musical, and difficult to distinguish from the wind as they flew. "Alas, my ancestors were a vile race beloved by Takhisis, and saw all others as servants and slaves. They brought humanity into bondage."

There was great sorrow in his voice as well as deep

regret. "In time the blackness of the ogre heart overcame our beauty and wisdom. As always, evil turned upon itself and destroyed the virtuous and good in us. We began to change. Our minds became polluted, our hearts deformed. Eventually even our physical appearance twisted to match the depravity of our souls. Our fall from grace was a rise to freedom for another people—humans."

He looked at Scamp and Dannika, who hugged her friend from behind as they flew so as not to fall, as she was still quite weak. She rested her chin on his shoulder, which made him feel all squiggly and squirmy inside, but in a nice way.

Then Anden looked at Mather and the platinum triangle that hung from his neck. It shone, but no brighter than the new peace and compassion Scamp saw in his older brother's eyes.

Anden looked at them all fondly, leaving out only Hedar. The dwarf didn't seem to mind, however. Holding tight to one of Patima's spines along her back, with arms and legs wrapped tightly and his eyes closed in terror, he didn't even appear to hear.

"Humans overthrew us," Anden said, "and won their freedom. But my people were too arrogant to accept this. We demanded that Takhisis restore our former beauty and power. But the Dark Queen, seeing our weakness, abandoned us, as she eventually does all who serve her." His voice deepened with loathing and disgust as he said, "So we turned to Morgion in our desperation."

"So that's where the spell came from," Mather said.

Anden nodded. "Morgion promised to restore our empire if we unleashed his magical plague upon dragons, the only beings free of his corrupting influence."

Patima growled viciously, though Scamp detected a tone of true fear in the sound as well. Recalling that fetid sludge behind her eyes, he couldn't blame her.

"Infected dragons would then be allowed to live in return for their slavery," Anden continued. "With a new, more powerful slave race, the empire would be restored. But before we could unleash his cursed plague, the human rebellion overthrew us once and for all."

"So, how did the tablet survive?" Scamp asked. "The stuff you're talking about happened hundreds of years ago, right?"

"Thousands," Anden said. "Before written record, other than that of the great historian Astinus, perhaps. How it survived, I am not certain, other than that I suspect Morgion protected it. I do know that during the time of the Kingpriest, when ogres were hunted and slaughtered simply for living, the tablet was captured and hidden away in the Temple of Istar. This is likely why it was never used—until Takhisis discovered the corrupted temple on the bottom of the Blood Sea and took it with her to the Abyss.

"There were two plans to deal with the metallic dragons during the recent war," Anden explained. "The first, which was carried out, was to steal the good dragons' eggs and blackmail them to stay out of the conflict."

Scamp felt Patima sob beneath him.

"A promise the Dark Queen did not keep," Anden said softly. "The stolen children were turned into draconians. But as horrid as this strategy was, the alternative was perhaps worse—to use Morgion's plague to enslave all dragons. Those who refused service would die. This, Morgion and his followers argued, would ensure Takhisis's victory: not only would the metallic dragons be enslaved on her side, but the chromatics would be forced to work together on pain of death, something they resisted the entire duration of the war."

"All dragons fighting in the dragonarmies," Scamp said, shuddering. It wasn't hard to imagine what might have come from that. He just pictured a world made of smoke and ash where nothing—absolutely nothing—lived. "Why didn't they do it? There's no way they would have lost."

"Because Takhisis did not want to grant Morgion such power," Anden explained. "The Gods of Evil trust each other less than any other beings. Takhisis feared that once he had rulership over dragons everywhere, Morgion would have the power not only to win the world, but to usurp her as well."

"One last question," Dannika said. Her voice was thin and strained, but at least she was talking again. "How did that horned ogre ever find out about the tablet?"

Anden's face grew grim. "I do not know. I did not even know that such beings still existed. After the fall of the empire, some of my people rejected the traditions of our fathers and left Ansalon. My people, the Irda, turned to Paladine to resist the base urges of our nature. We have lived, isolated and peaceful, under his protection ever since. But another group left this continent as well. They followed a powerful cultist of Morgion, who initially was granted the spell of the dragon plague. They traveled even farther than we Irda, beyond the known world. We had always assumed they all perished."

"You assumed wrong," Patima said. Scamp felt her body rumble beneath him with every syllable. "There are things in this world beyond your dreams, Irda, and others beyond your nightmares."

Anden nodded solemnly. "I should have known something like this would happen. In a dream, Paladine appeared to me as a platinum rain and gave me the geas to reclaim the tablet. I never considered that a dark god may have made a similar quest for a follower of his across the sea."

"But how did Pug's mom get it?" Scamp asked, hugging Pug.

"Perhaps he was to be an experiment," Anden offered.

"A first test, too young and weak to resist the spell."

"So his mom died to protect him," Scamp said. Nuzzling the wyrmling, he whispered, "I told you your mom loved you."

Anden looked away and did not comment.

Scamp was so engrossed in the story and sensations of flight that he realized where he was only when Patima dipped in the air, and steadying her wings, glided toward the ground. There, just over a wooded hill, was Tarban. To the east, signs of the fire were still clear. He could even make out the clearing that had once been the Bristling Briar, though he was too far away to see if the dragon's body still lay there. He was home.

He looked at the tiny wyrmling asleep in his arms. Home was another world, a world where dragons were evil and unwanted, and could never be loved by a boy. Scamp hugged Pug and tried not to cry.

When Patima landed, they all slid from her back. Mather helped Dannika dismount, while Anden had to carry Hedar. The dwarf, with his eyes still closed, screamed and fought and kicked, insisting that they were all going to fall to their deaths. Scamp was pretty sure he even bit the graceful ogre. When the pair was on the ground—Hedar, pale faced and sweating, and Anden holding his arm—the two looked worse for wear than after the battle with the ogre mage.

Scamp dismounted last, still hugging the baby in his arms. He saw them all looking at him sadly.

"Come on," Dannika said to the still shivering dwarf.

"Come where?" Hedar demanded.

"Would you like to meet Peda?"

Hedar appraised her. "Didn't you say he's dead?"

"He is," she said, and though her voice was sad, there was peace in it as well. "But that doesn't mean he's lost to me."

Looking thoughtful, the dwarf nodded. When the pair started away, Mather said, "I'll come as well. I have my own thanks to offer." As he passed Scamp, he took his brother's shoulder and squeezed. They both looked at the sleeping wyrmling. Mather quickly looked elsewhere. "I'm sorry, Scamp." He walked away.

Anden approached Scamp, his marble cheeks stern and cold. "It's time the wyrmling is dealt with."

Scamp sheltered Pug in his arms. "He's mine. I'll take care of him and he'll be good, you'll see."

"The wyrmling is evil, Scamp," Anden said. "It is not his fault. He was made thus."

"So were you," Scamp shot back. "You're just a pretty ogre, and nothing's more evil than an ogre."

"We Irda changed," Anden replied.

"He can change too!"

Patima had been watching the baby sleep. Her gaze was distant, clouded with fondness and pleasant memories. Hearing their discussion, she said, "Please, give me my child. I've missed him so much."

Anden looked at the broken-hearted dragon sadly. He shook his head. "He is not your child and can never be. When he grows older, he will kill you if he can."

"You think this is worse than eternity alone?"

Scamp thought desperately for any excuse to save the wyrmling. He couldn't think of anything that would convince Anden. In a last, desperate effort, he remembered the tablet. If he could snatch back the spell maybe he could hold it hostage until the Irda agreed to leave Pug safe.

He studied Anden, paying particular attention to the tablet tucked into the beautiful ogre's belt. He was judging when to make a grab for it when the stark contrast of the tablet's colors struck him—black and white, one as dark as Nuitari, the other pure as starlight.

And he knew what to do.

"Use the spell!" he said, excitedly.

"What spell?" Anden asked.

Scamp pointed to the tablet. "You said this spell takes dragons' wills, enslaves them. What about the other side, the white one? Does it do the opposite?"

Patima's rich rumble added, "The boy is correct. All magic has its opposite."

Anden covered the tablet with his hand, as if to hide it. "I'm sorry, it isn't possible."

"Why?" Scamp demanded.

"The inverse of the spell does grant a dragon free will, but I cannot cast it. No one can. It requires that the caster honestly believe the recipient of the spell has a good soul."

"What so hard about that?" Scamp asked.

"Because I know chromatic dragons," Anden said grimly. "I know the monstrous Red that nearly destroyed our island home." He looked at Patima, who averted her gaze. "You know your evil cousins who killed your mate and helped steal your children. Even you," he said to Scamp, "have seen the devastation wrought by the dragonarmies. None of us truly believe that these dragons could ever be anything but what they are—vicious and evil. And a caster who does not believe in the goodness of the dragon will find himself enslaved to the beast. The magic must force a choice: either grant choice to the dragon, or take choice from the caster."

Scamp looked at the wyrmling sleeping in his arms. Since his adventure began, Scamp had saved lives: Dannika's, Mather's, Anden's, his own, and who knew who else by thwarting the ogre mage's attempt to enslave an army of dragons. But he'd failed to save others. Peda. The White Robes who bravely protected them at the academy. The wyrmling's mother, even.

Suddenly Scamp knew why Mather had always been reluctant to try to help him—because of fear of failure. He thought of Mather trying to save Grandpa and having to watch him hang. His brother had found the courage to try again.

Did Scamp have the courage to try now? It all hinged on one question: did he believe the wyrmling was truly good?

"I will cast the spell," Scamp said.

Anden stared at him as if he doubted his hearing. Even Patima was watching nervously.

"Are you sure?" the Irda said.

Scamp nodded.

"If the wyrmling has an evil soul you'll be enslaved to him," Anden said sternly, "as Patima was to the cultist of Morgion. But as this is done of your own will, the magic cannot be undone. There is no way back. Are you sure?"

Scamp felt cold, dizzy, and as if his bones had all turned to jam. Despite it all, the one thing he did not feel was doubt.

"How do I start?" he asked.

Anden appraised him a moment. Then, with a single nod, he held out the tablet, white side up. "Place your hand on the tablet and repeat after me." Anden began to chant.

Scamp placed his hand on the stone. Its touch was smooth, almost like glass. He repeated what Anden said.

The words were strange and full, as if made to fit mouths bigger than a human's. His tongue felt like it was tripping when he tried to emulate the gruff, choking syllables never used in human language. But he pressed through any mistakes he made, refusing to question himself, refusing to doubt.

And as he chanted, the wyrmling in his arm began to glow. It was a strange light, intense but dim, at once both dark and light.

As the glow intensified Scamp could feel himself being pulled, sucked at as if by a powerful river's rush. The dragon was trying to suck him in. Instinct told him to resist, to halt the chanting until he felt safe once more. He refused.

The sensation grew more powerful. Light began to flicker and bend, warping as it swirled toward the radiant wyrmling. The edges of Scamp's vision wavered black and began to pulse in time with his thundering heart. His world began to swirl and narrow, closing in around him.

Then he felt a whisper on his cheek, and the touch of a warm scale. "Please, save my child. I believe in you."

Bolstered by these words, Scamp raised his voice and chanted more strongly than before. He felt himself falling into the dragon, and beyond, into nothing, and did not fight it. He believed.

The aura around Pug flickered, as if catching fire,

then flared. A radiant bronze light, bright as the sun, filled Scamp's vision. The light filled him as well. He could feel it moving through him, bursting through flesh and blood and bone. As he felt his body disappear, washed away by the light, he felt the touch of Patima's head on his shoulder. It was here the light sprang from, her molten eyes. It ended in the wyrmling, building until the tiny dragon looked as if he were made of luminescence.

Scamp was the pathway between the two, and he felt himself being used up in the process. As the light grew so blinding it turned dark, and the rush of power through him slowed, Scamp looked at the wyrmling in his arm. Nudged from sleep, Pug slowly opened his eyes—shining, molten bronze eyes.

Scamp laughed with the voice of a dragon and wept metallic tears of joy as he lost consciousness.

When Scamp awoke he was alone. There were huge footprints in the clearing around him, but no sign of Patima or Anden. Or Pug.

Panicking, Scamp rose and searched the clearing. Nothing.

Had it worked? Was Pug free to live his life as he chose, good instead of evil? Scamp certainly hoped so. He had no wish to live as a slave for the rest of his life.

Then the wind whispered to him: *The child is free. Thank you.*

"Patima?" He looked around and saw no one. "Where are you? Don't leave me!"

Our world and yours are different, and different they must stay. It is best for mortals when dragons are little more than dreams.

"But I want my dreams to be real."

So they are. You will be thought of with fondness and love, and my child will know of all you did for us both. He will grow to dream of the hero you are. And when you dream in turn, you will meet again, and this will be as real as life, and more real than the waking world. Until this time, thank you, and fare you well, little Scamp.

The voice was gone. And though Scamp missed it he did not mourn because he believed the promise, and knew that the things in dreams could sometimes be more real than life.

"Is everything all right?" It was his brother's voice. Turning, Scamp saw Mather and Dannika standing at the edge of the clearing, watching him with clear worry.

"What happened?" Dannika asked.

Scamp considered for a moment before saying, "You wouldn't believe me if I told you." Then he smiled, letting them know all they needed.

Danni smiled in return. "Then your parents won't either, but you may as well come tell them. And us, while you're at it."

"I don't know," Mather said sternly. "They'll probably think you're fibbing and wash your mouth out with soap. Frankly, considering the past, I wouldn't blame them." Turning on his heel, Mather started walking toward the village.

Scamp's smile wilted. "But you'd tell them I'm telling the truth, right?" Mather continued to walk. "Right?"

Mather disappeared into the foliage without looking back. Then, from a distance, he called, "Of course. You know I've got your back."

Dannika shot Scamp a small, knowing smile. "I think I'll start the story with you standing in your underwear and boots outside of town. I can't wait until your parents hear that!" With that, she dashed into the forest and toward home, anxious to pay her friend back for all the mischief he had caused her in the past. Oh, well, Scamp decided. She'd earned it.

So Scamp started walking back to Tarban, knowing that his adventures were not over after all. He had seen dragons and evil ogres from across the sea. He had fought battles, saved lives, and cast a powerful spell. And a green dragon—a good dragon—waited to share friendship in his dreams.

With all this in mind, he almost hoped to meet Jaiben when he walked into the village. If he did, he promised he would admit that the bully wasn't the ugliest ogre in the world after all.

About the Author

R.D. Henham is a scribe in the great library of Palanthas. In the course of transcribing stories of legendary dragons, the author felt a gap existed in the story of the everydragon: ordinary dragons who end up doing extraordinary things. With the help of fellow scribes, R.D. has filled that gap with this series of books based on Sindri Suncatcher's remarkable *A Practical Guide to Dragons*.

About the Author's Assistant

Clint Johnson resides in Salt Lake City, Utah, where he was born and raised. He doesn't care particularly where he dies so long as it is a considerable time in the future. This is his first novel written for children. For more information about Clint and his work, or writing and life (his or yours or in general), visit www.clintjohnsonwrites.com.

**Fly through the air with the greatest of ease—
on a silver dragon!**

Jace, a high-wire acrobat in a traveling circus, thought he knew
the thrill of adventure. But when he meets Belen, a strange girl
with no memory of her past, he soon discovers how much more
adventure—and danger—awaits him. Not long after Belen joins
the circus, a wizard arrives and stops the show—not by magic,
but by accusation. Belen is not human, he says: she is a dragon
who destroyed a nearby town. As Jace and Belen set off in a race
against time to clear Belen's name and recover her memory, mysterious forces conspire to throw them off track. Can Jace learn
to fly through the air with the greatest of ease on the back of a
dragon before time runs out? Find out in:

SILVER
DRAGON CODEX

OPEN UP A WORLD OF ADVENTURE WITH THE

ROLEPLAYING GAME STARTER SET

RUN THE GAME

Build your own dungeons and pit your friends
against monsters and villains!

PLAY THE GAME

Explore the dungeon with your friends,
fight the monsters, and bring back the treasure!

GRAB SOME FRIENDS

AND THE

STARTER SET

AND

START PLAYING TODAY

playdnd.com